LONG NIGHT AT LAKE NEVER

Eric David Roman

a Wholly Roman Publication

Long Night at Lake Never

© 2022 Eric David Roman
Cover Art © 2022 Travis Falligant
ISBN: 9798830525619
2nd Edition

This is a work of a fiction, obviously. Names, characters, places, and incidents are either the product of the author's
imagination, or are used fictitiously. Any resemblance to actual living persons or dead, business establishments, events, or locales, is purely coincidental.

Warnings: Graphic violence/gore.
Homophobia. Abuse. Bullying. Hate groups.
Murder. Past trauma. Religious shaming. Suicide.

For Brandi, who left us too soon.

<u>Author's note:</u>

It would be remiss of me if we did not take a moment before getting into the fictional horrific fun of *Long Night at Lake Never* to discuss the real-life horror of conversion/reparative therapies aimed at LGBTQ youth. For many, it's an all too real experience, and queer youth who undergo conversion therapy are two times more likely to take their own life (per the Trevor Project's 2019 survey). Currently the practice is fully banned in only twenty states. But I hope, after enjoying my story, you will spend a moment and see where your state, county, or city stands on conversion therapy. And where you can help, or whom you can vote for that will bring awareness to the issue. While I may love to write about the horrific, the dark, and generally creepier side of life, I wholeheartedly believe in a future that's a beautiful and accepting place for everyone...well, except assholes.

E.D.R.

God Hates Faggs

Tyler Wills had not gazed out the car's window for a solid hour, but when he finally did, those three words angrily mocked him. Each word with its own crudely hand-painted sign, and each one staked in the ground along the roadside. The message, along with the overall cheap tackiness of the signs, churned his stomach.

And they couldn't even spell it right. Assholes.

After tilting his head back, he nestled against the leather headrest of his father's Mercedes and rolled his eyes, thinking about life and its accompanying bullshit. How much he wanted to be free—eighteen was ten months away. How much easier everything would be once on his own. Life, his way. A glance out the window and another sign met his eyes, this one reflective green.

It announced they were twenty-five miles from their destination: Camp Horizons. The crude signs, which at first appeared random, now made more sense. Tyler could have groaned or sighed loudly, but no one cared or listened. His parents remained silent the entire three-hour trip, and no noises Ty made were going to change that fact in the last thirty minutes. No radio. No small talk. Only the car's interior noises, their collective breathing, and the curt driving directions of the British-voiced GPS.

Nadine Wills sat stone-faced and stared out the windshield, only letting the occasional sniffle escape her nose to show she was still alive. Tyler expected a ride filled with screaming and admonishments against his character, but instead, he got the Wills silent treatment. In the two weeks since the night Tyler was brought home by the police, she hadn't acknowledged him once.

She did not listen to him that night either. Once the door opened and she saw Ty there looking small and pitiful with the bulky police officer behind him, she slapped his face and demanded he go to his room. He didn't, remaining hidden on the stairwell, giggling to himself, as the cop explained to his parents their seventeen-year-old son had been caught in the park giving, as the officer described, "*vigorous* oral sex." He emphasized the word vigorous multiple times, either driving home the point he'd witnessed the offensive act, or to show how impressed he'd been by the skills displayed but remained obligated to uphold the law.

Tyler lamented life was not more like porn. If his had been, the cop would gladly have joined in, and Tyler wouldn't have faced his third strike with Michael and Nadine. The previous two were for his attitude, minor offensives, but this infraction came with the threat of an indecent exposure charge, for which he got let go with only a warning. However, the more significant issue was the revelation their only son was queer. He knew the ordeal would cost him this time, which it did.

One day after the incident, as the event became referred to, Michael barged into Tyler's room, a disgusted look etched into his worn and wrinkled face, and his laptop clenched in his hands. Tyler rolled his eyes as his red-faced father, livid at his only son for being a filthy fucking cocksucker (his exact words), showed him the website for Camp Horizons, a "rehabilitation" center for homosexual youth. Tyler understood exactly what a pray-the-gay-away-style conversion camp consisted of. He was an educated young man and was aware of what kind of rehab went down at places like those.

The blood drained from his face as Michael smirked at Ty's horrified reaction. Nadine wasn't present for Michael's fiery antihomo tirade about how the camp would be healthy for him. Tyler figured a silent *or else* came attached to the demand he agreed to. He hoped Nadine would swoop in for a rescue, tell her husband he was being ridiculous as she had in the past and that would all be fixed.

But Ty didn't count on her this time; he knew she wouldn't leave the safety of the bedroom where the surplus of Xanax kept her numbed and staring at the ceiling in mindless wonderment.

The week until they left for the camp had been hell. They took everything from him: The car went first, the phone next, along with all the electronics, and like a prisoner, his remaining freedoms were stripped away. Tyler spent the week locked in his near-empty bedroom. The severity of his punishment pissed him off and it wasn't due to premarital sex or getting caught by the police.

If he'd been blown by a girl, sure there would have been some yelling and tears since Nadine cried at fucking everything. But once she settled, his father would have come into his room and congratulated him on becoming a man and probably expunged any punishment with a hearty high-five.

No, their anger, their disgust came from the fact Tyler was gay. What infuriated them more, Ty had no issue with his sexuality at all. To them, being queer equaled unacceptable, and yet, he held no shame whatsoever. For the past two years, he'd tried on multiple occasions to come out but always retreated at the last minute. He understood the truth: Michael and Nadine were bigoted archaic assholes. The kind who spoke disparagingly about queer people whenever they showed up on a television show or in a movie. "Ugh, do we need more of *them?*" Nadine would say as she fidgeted in her spot until the offensive parties left the screen. His father would mumble *fags* under his breath, and so Tyler would sit there being hurt and annoyed by the two people who were supposed to love him more than anything.

And he thought, foolishly, he could make it to eighteen and get out before he ever had to tell them. His libido thought otherwise. The allegations were true. He'd done everything the cop accused him of—and more—before the offensive flashlight so rudely shined on them in the plastic playhouse atop the slide. Tyler picked at the seams on his jeans and thought about Daniel, his long-time crush, who had finally agreed to meet him.

Closing his eyes he pictured Daniel's slender face, his deep eyes, and his full lips, which felt as nice as Ty had hoped. Without any of his devices, there'd been no way to see how much trouble Daniel had gotten into with his family. And no means to apologize or tell him how he'd not stopped thinking about their brief night. Nadine and Michael hadn't merely sent Tyler away; they'd successfully cut him off from the world. He wouldn't know if there may have been something more with Daniel than a few quick make-out sessions behind the lunchroom and a sloppy half-finished blow job.

He opened his eyes when his father's voice demanded he wake up though he had not been sleeping. A large wooden sign filled the front windshield as they passed, declaring they'd reached Camp Horizons. In the camp's heyday, the hand-carved sign had been brightly painted with yellows and blues depicting a serene sun setting on a group of cabins. Each ray of the sun became a cross the closer to the camp they reached, but the current state of the sign showed those days were long gone. Now the sign's faded paint showed off how dried and cracked the wood had become. The sign hung crooked, drooping on one side from damage to one of the posts, which no one had bothered to fix. Past the broken sign were a few hundred more feet of dense forest, which sent a chill, cold and icy, traversing up Tyler's spine and sent shudders through his body.

The camp was more isolated than he realized, and the fact unsettled him. An apprehensive knot formed in his chest and told him this place wasn't right.

The Mercedes followed the curve of the camp's driveway, and Tyler saw a trio of cabins nestled together along the rim of the circular drive. Behind them, sloping down the uneven terrain to the edge of Lake Never were several more. From the window, Tyler spotted a round-faced man in his late thirties, with a short beard and thinning hair, wearing a bright-yellow shirt and tan khakis, waving happily at them. Michael pulled the car around until he faced the way they'd come in. He shoved the gearshift into park, pissed off at it and blaming everything in the world for his son being a queer.

Michael turned to face Tyler in the backseat. For a moment, Ty thought his father would finally speak to him, and he did, but not with any words. The anger and disappointment were painted all over his face as they'd been for days, and the look told Tyler without question, *you'd better not fuck this up too*. Tyler blew him a kiss and flung his car door open, happy for the fresh air. As his parents slammed their doors, the man from the porch trotted down to them.

"The Lord has blessed us with a beautiful day, hasn't he? Hello, Mr. and Mrs. Wills. Welcome to Camp Horizons," he said warmly, his greeting coated thickly by a Southern accent as rich as syrup smothering a stack of pancakes. He extended his hand and shook Michael's, and then Nadine's, who barely registered a response.

"Robert Kendall, the camp director here at Horizons. But please, Bob is fine. Been going by it for years. And this young man must be Tyler." Bob swung his hand over to Tyler, an obviously super fake grin smeared across his round face.

Tyler refused to shake any hands. Instead, he let his focus drift around the camp as Bob spoke to his parents. If Horizons had any glory days, they were long gone. There was not one cabin which didn't need some form of repair or wasn't boarded up. Every surface needed a paint job, and the grounds were overgrown, except in the prominent areas along the front to keep the entrance looking deceptively beautiful. Tyler's sneakers dug into the gravel of the drive, his thoughts only on running away, as Bob led them to the office sitting to the left of the largest cabin, which he referred to as Integrity Cabin.

For a religiously run camp, Tyler found there was not much around touting the place's pious nature past the crosses on the camp's entrance sign. In his head, he half expected to see nothing but crosses—hung to everything, twenty feet tall—but the camp appeared subdued.

He recanted this opinion once inside Bob's office. The room was adorned with an obscenely large and ornately framed painting of Jesus Christ on the rear wall. Between the pictures of the camp through the years were photos of the Guides who had worked there, small but ornate crosses, placards with scripture quotes, and religious-themed motivational posters, which encouraged all to Pray it Away with the power of God.

Situated at his desk, Bob was tiny in front of the looming Jesus, who glared down on them, and the desk was covered with files, papers, and a complete set of apostle bobbleheads.

The Wills family sat quietly as Bob beamed at them with a righteous awkwardness for a silent minute. Exhaling loudly, he leaned his head up to the heavens as he began, "The Lord is here today.

Yes, he is. He is always present when one of his disciples begins their *Journey*." The word, said often, was always accompanied with a pompous weighted reverence. "Tyler, Horizons exists to restore those trapped within sexual sin. Our program is specifically designed to cater to those that have fallen prey to the sinful cult of homosexuality." He bowed his head, raised his right hand, and shook like an evangelist on Sunday morning television, casting away queerness like one would cast off the evil eye.

"Homosexuality is a vile disease, and through the power of prayer, we can get Tyler onto the path of righteousness and return him to the arms of our Lord."

"Kinda thought the idea here would be getting me *out* of the arms of men, but hey, who am I to argue?" Tyler could do nothing but laugh off the absurdity around him.

"God sees you, Tyler Wills, and your soul is in peril. Do you want to spend eternity in damnation and hellfire? Let's try to approach this with some decorum. *Our* mission here is to save your soul."

Tyler rolled his eyes at the idea of his soul needing saving—an impulse reaction but one that earned him a hard smack across the back of his head from his father.

"How long does this process take, making them straight again?" Michael asked with an annoyed tone, suggesting he expected to literally drop the offensive party off and leave. Nadine sat quietly, not looking at her son, husband, or Bob's suntanned face. She stared up at the large painting of Jesus, dopey eyed in her sedated state. "Tyler had an incident," she whispered softly.

"I got caught vigorously sucking some cock," Tyler boasted as his father fumed, and Nadine covered her mouth and shook her head.

"An *incident*," Michael spoke over him, "that concerned us enough to bring him here for treatment."

Bob put his hands together in a prayer stance and once again sounded like a preacher. "The path to religious righteousness is a thorny one. Romans 12 tells us, '*Rejoice in hope, be patient in tribulation, be constant in prayer.*'" He quoted the Bible with the slimy ease of a used car salesman trying to offload a lemon.

Michael rudely cut through the religious platitudes. "And what kind of time frame does that entail?"

"Bob," Tyler interjected before the camp director answered, "my parents are extremely uncomfortable. Neither of them is religious enough to know what Romans means. What they want you to tell them, and in the simplest words possible, is how long this introduction will take. They're so uncomfortable. I mean, look at how much they want to leave." The retort was worth the second smack to the head.

"The *Journey* is two and a half weeks, but they are laborious weeks for sure." Bob cleared his throat. "Now I'm required to make clear that neither I nor my Guides are actually licensed therapists. We're merely servants of God, who've gone through the *Journey* and are invested in keeping the camp running so other young people will have a safe space to embark on their own path back to the Lord."

He rattled off a few other disclaimers rapidly before sliding across the desk three papers he advised were confidentiality agreements, each stating the Wills would not divulge their therapeutic techniques.

Tyler figured his father listened and honed in, as Tyler had, on the unlicensed and unregulated part, which to anyone else would have been a huge red flag. He hoped that would have shown his father how ludicrous the entire idea was, and how potentially dangerous. Except Tyler imagined his father hoped the so-called techniques included a little bit of physical punishment.

"Fucking kill them all, and we wouldn't have this problem," Michael Wills had once proclaimed at the breakfast table in front of his son and wife after becoming annoyed with the ongoing coverage over the fight for marriage equality.

"We here at Horizons have developed our own patent-pending, seven-step rehabilitation program, which will take Tyler on a voyage of self-discovery where he will once again find, through prayer, and our assistance, God's eternal love.
And in that love, he will find the courage to reject these deviant homosexual impulses, falsely implanted within him by Satan.

"All of our Guides have taken the *Journey*. They are trained to assist other young men and women going through the process. Luckily for Tyler, our attendance is rather low this cycle, which is all the better to give those here a truly one-on-one, immersive experience, which will return him to our Lord and Savior. Through God's beautiful bounty, we are blessed to be here providing this service to his flock."

"I'm pretty sure this shit is illegal." Tyler's already upset stomach tied itself in more knots listening to the eerie way Bob referred to God so subserviently that it didn't seem to Tyler like they had the healthiest relationship. Whomever Bob was referring to wasn't the God Ty knew, and everyone in the room would be gutted to know how well Tyler was versed with the Bible, but he kept that to himself.

"Language," Bob chided. "We keep our words G-rated at Horizons."

"Fine, I'll reiterate—isn't conversion therapy illegal?"

"No laws have been passed as of yet...in this state anyway," Bob quickly pointed out smugly before shifting his attention to Michael and Nadine. "As you may have observed driving in, Lake Never is rather large. We are secluded here on the south side. As such, there is no access to the internet. No televisions. No radios. No distractions. And any fraternizing, in a physical manner, is strictly forbidden."

Tyler sat back in his chair, believing he had found his way out. The first guy he found to be willing—bam—he'd get kicked out.

"Expulsion is not the punishment," Bob declared as if reading the blueprints of Tyler's escape plan directly off his face. "The program resets, and our Journeyer must begin again. And if this causes them to go over their allotted time, there will of course be a small fee. We will need to collect Tyler's phone and any other electronic devices he may have. There is a landline here in my office. If you are so inclined to check on Tyler's progress, you may call, but the Journeyers are not permitted access to it."

Tyler laughed. They wouldn't give a shit about his progress once they drove off. "Don't have to worry about that, Bob. These assholes don't care if they hear from their faggy son or not."

"Language." Bob's demeanor flipped, and the word came with a more pointed tone making it clear foul language wouldn't be tolerated again.

"Tyler, shut up," his father demanded. "And after these two weeks he will be straight, correct?"

"Oh yes," Bob assured Michael. "We here at Horizons are God's mechanics, determined to help fix our brothers and sisters who've been led astray."

"There is nothing fucking wrong with me. I happened to luck out and got these two braindead assholes for parents." Tyler went to stand up and storm out. Michael proved quicker, snatching his arm roughly, forcing him down into his seat.

"Sit the fuck down right now," Michael yelled, never once looking at his son. "You will take this seriously. You will follow the rules, and you will not come home until—"

"Until what?" Tyler pulled his arm back. "Until I magically like pussy? There is nothing wrong with me the way I am."

Michael wound up his hand again and started to say something when Bob jumped in. "Mr. Wills, please. Tyler, we will not accept this kind of talk or behavior at Horizons. That is no way to speak to your parents. One of the commandments is to honor thy mother and father. They are your moral compass."

"You're fucking joking, right?" Tyler sat up in

the chair and laughed. "Moral compass? My mother over there dopes herself every day to ignore the fact that my father is sticking his dick into every woman he meets. She doesn't care about this as long as her meds are refilled, and the credit card doesn't get declined. I do believe gluttony, infidelity, and generally being a shitty person are sins too, are they not? Where's the rehab camp for these asses?"

Nadine shifted in her seat and exhaled loudly as she turned her face away when Michael sent the back of his hand across Tyler's face, effectively silencing him. Bob didn't comment on the slap, waiting a moment until the air settled before he continued.

"We are not here to discuss semantics, Tyler. We're here to talk about you starting your *Journey* toward being a straight and God-fearing member of society."

Tyler rubbed the side of his face, still hot from Michael's hand, and shrugged the slap off. "I get your gig; you pick and choose what parts of the Bible you feel like enforcing. The rest doesn't matter, right?"

Bob, still sporting his Cheshire-cat-like phony grin, studied Tyler as he slid the confidential agreement across the desk toward Michael. Bob motioned to the pens in the cup in front of him. "We are going to require our fee up front."

☠

The official Guides' uniform at Horizons consisted of a canary-yellow polo shirt with the words Camp

Horizons and the same logo from the entrance sign in a small square, stitched in a soft-blue thread on the left breast and khaki pants.

Those bright shirts were what made Guides Matt and Killian easy to spot as they made their way along one of the older trails. Matt stopped, unsure why. The beautiful foliage and tress surrounding them grew more serene and peaceful the further from camp the trail traveled. But the forest also grew denser, and that dense collection of trees worked overtime to make Matt inexplicably nervous.

There were always tales about Lake Never, the kind circling in hushed whispers and bedtime stories. There were trails you weren't supposed to traverse, and areas where one should never camp, but those were just stories. However, he was sure he spotted a dark flash of something, through the trees along the trail—a something he believed to be large, human, and following them.

"Why'd you stop?" Killian asked, annoyed to find Matt lagging a few feet behind him, staring off into the forest.

"I thought I saw something," Matt explained. He would never have come out this far if not pushed by Killian to do so. The Guide had been relentless pushing them to go further along the trail. Matt peered through the thick branches and brush, trying to catch a second glimpse of the flash he'd seen.

"What did this thing look like?"

Killian stepped up behind Matt without him realizing. "I'm not sure, kinda like a flash, maybe something like a person...maybe."

"I knew it." The twenty-four-year-old Killian had gone on daily rounds to check the lesser-used cabins since he'd first spotted a figure by the toolshed, but the shape moved fast, and Killian had failed to catch him. The perpetrator was a person; there was no doubt about that. No animal, even a bear, appeared as a tall, broad-shouldered man bundled in layers of clothing, covered by a hoodie. Killian had theorized at dinner the night before, and again over breakfast that morning his certainty that if the mysterious person walked to and from Horizons, then their camp was based somewhere close and along the trail.

"Is that why you pushed us to come all the way out here, your mysterious stranger theory?"

"Yes." Killian's answer was firm. "I know what I saw, and I think they were wearing those clothes that went missing last month. Someone is camping out here, and I'm going to find him."

Matt threw out a final glance to the spot he'd been focused on and broke away.

He wanted to leave, but Killian's insistence on the intruder being real, plus the *flash* of whatever it had been behind the tree line, succeeded in creeping him out. "Can we head back now?"

The fact Killian urged them to come out so far simply to investigate the supposed intruder bummed him out. There had been a lot of thoughts running through Matt's head during their hike. Despite his reformed ex-gay status and the fact he now guided others along their *Journey*, the only reason Matt agreed to keep going was for the alone time with the cute Killian. After learning togetherness wasn't why their walk went past its usual half mile, Matt became a party mix of disappointment, self-loathing, and repressed horniness. All covered with a generous dose of shame sprinkled over the top.

Killian agreed the time had come to head back. "Lemme go answer the call of nature, and we'll get out of here. I've not seen anything." Excusing himself, he veered off down an embankment and stepped a good ways away from the trail and Matt.

At the first thickest tree he could find, Killian undid his pants while thinking about the restraint he had shown in not calling out his walking companion for the continuous glances that were being thrown his way. Looks that suggested Matt hoped for something *other* than walking. He was flattered—Matt was handsome, and really funny, and Killian enjoyed their walks—but "gay is not the way" as Bob constantly preached to them. The idea of them being far from the prying eyes of the other Guides filled the air with temptation, but Killian, ever devout, chastised himself. Those were not the thoughts of a straight, God-fearing man. Wrapped up in hating himself for harboring feelings of wanting to kiss Matt longer than he should have, Killian was unaware of the tall mysterious figure stepping up behind him.

Killian shook his dick a couple of times, and once sure he'd dodged any of those last-minute drips that would have lingered on his pants, tiny betrayers of his private act, he zipped up. The hairs stood on his neck and arms as chills raced through his blood. He continued to stare ahead at the peeling bark of the tree, wondering what Matt's next move would be.

There was, no lie, that part of him hoped for Matt to slide up around him and take his manhood in his hands, but the other part wanted him to do nothing. In fact, Killian hoped for nothing, he'd already decided to turn him in for misconduct if he did, a decision which did not change when a hand grabbed his neck. Killian realized instantly the touch wasn't the tender embrace of a nervous would-be lover. Before he went to smack the hand away, the grip tightened and forced him forward. His head bashed against the tree trunk in front of him.

The blow ripped open a three-inch-long gash along his forehead, which gushed with blood. Killian was released. Dazed, he fell to the ground. Looking up, he half expected to see Matt's big green eyes, but instead saw the Man, his face obscured up to his eyes, which were shadowed by the hood of the jacket. Killian crawled away as fast as his spinning head would let him. He went off in what he believed was the direction of the trail and away from his assailant. The blood from his wound painted his face, making him appear as if he were in the cheering section at a football game, and burned his eyes, forcing him to squint, unable to realize he'd fled in the wrong direction. Pushing himself along the ground, he cursed himself for feeling the need to walk so far away to urinate.

The Man stalked his prey like a lion preparing to take down an injured gazelle, making no sounds as he moved closer. Stepping up behind Killian, he raised his heavy boot and slammed it down onto Killian's lower back. As he continued to press hard, the Man mashed his foot on Killian's spine like someone snuffing out a lit cigarette until he heard the snap of his vertebrae. The Guide's pained howl sent the birds fluttering away from their tress in dis-

-tress. Matt paced with nervousness on the trail, fighting the urge to sneak away and catch a peek of Killian. No amount of prayer prevented the Guide from thinking about seeing the six-foot-tall, dark-haired Adonis naked, if only to get a glimpse of the goods, which who wouldn't? Matt knew he would be spending extra time on his knees that evening— praying for forgiveness. The fluttering wings and distressed cries of those same birds as they raced away from their trees caught Matt's attention and he paused, trying to locate where the scream originated from and if it was Killian's. He rushed over to where the birds had departed from, calling out the Guide's name.

Killian resumed trying to wiggle away, dragging himself by his hands, no longer able to feel any part of his lower extremities. "Don't," he mumbled, attempting to warn his friend who sounded close. His throat had been bruised from being grabbed, his voice now too weak to carry. But Matt had already slid down the embankment toward him. With the blood still flooding his eyes, he appeared as nothing but a blurry form, reaching out for Killian. The Guide wished he'd not pushed to come so far to investigate, but laments were a moot point now. Trying to wipe the blood from his face and eyes, he found his wound continued to flow unabated.

Matt's eyes were wide with fear, which jettisoned into concern the moment he found Killian struggling to move on the ground. Kneeling by him, Matt extended his hand out while staring in shock at the large open wound on the Guide's head. "Holy shitake mushrooms, Killian what happened?"

Matt hadn't heard anyone behind him. The blow he received to his dome proved to be a surprise, one he didn't fully register until he was face down on the ground and being hoisted back up off his feet. The Man held Matt up off the forest floor as if he weighed no more than ten pounds and rushed him up against the nearest tree. Revealing a hunting knife in his free hand, the Man jabbed the tip at Matt, taunting the young man who begged to be released.

Pressing the blade's tip against the *C* in the word Camp on Matt's shirt, he dragged the knife across the camp's name and logo until he reached the end and started over, digging the knife in deeper as he pulled the blade across Matt's chest as if crossing something off his to-do list. Each slice opened the wound further. The blood ran down his chest, soaking his yellow shirt. When the logo met its demise, the Man held the blade firmly at eye level and sprung forward, driving the knife through Matt's left shoulder and deep into the thick trunk with a loud *shunk*.

Pinned like a bug on a display board in science class, Matt struggled but was unable to do anything except call out for help which would never come. The mysterious Man, this violent creature who, in Matt's opinion, came straight out of hell, had grabbed Killian by his thick black hair and threw him over the stump of a knocked-over tree. Taking a moment, he arranged Killian, who no longer had the energy to fight back, into position—execution-style. After aligning his neck with the edge of the stump, the Man picked up his axe resting next to it and raised the weapon high above his head.

"Why are you are doing this?" Matt begged the Man to stop and tried to turn his head away, but the simple motion sent throngs of pain through him. Without a moment's hesitation, the Man heaved the blade down with a stunning amount of force.

The axe, old and rusted from years of neglect, buried itself into the flesh of Killian's neck but did not slice all the way through. The blade stopped short a quarter of the way in. From the crude opening, blood spurted and bubbled up with the grandeur of a garden pebble fountain. Killian's protests were nothing but garbled and incoherent noise. The Man, not pleased with his instrument, tossed the axe down and repositioned himself in front of the stump. His boot rose over the flowing wound in Killian's neck.

"Oh God, please don't." Matt's cries for help, the passionate pleas to his Lord and savior, pleading for Jesus to swoop in and save them, went unanswered. Killian's attempts to grab at the ground beneath him with twitchy hands that were unable to take hold were futile. The Man let his raised right foot linger a moment before dropping the heel on Killian's neck.

Matt, unable to keep praying, mustered screams instead as he grabbed at the knife's handle, frantically trying to remove it. The killer's foot shot up into the air again, and Matt clamped his eyes closed. The knife would not budge, and he knew he hadn't the strength to remove the blade from the tree. His eyes remained closed as the second, and then third and final blow sent a loud crunch reverberating in his ears. The Man had successfully stomped through Killian's neck. Once it hit the ground, Killian's decapitated head rolled away from his body and the stump and into some bushes.

Praying harder than when he'd tried to cure himself of his homosexual affliction two years prior, Matt implored God for the strength to do what he needed. The Man, occupied with retrieving the head, turned away, and the moment proved to be Matt's only window for escape. Taking a deep breath and planting his feet on the ground, he steadied himself against the trunk and pushed. Biting his lip, he subdued the pained screams as the knife moved through shoulder the more he forced himself away from the tree. The handle hurt the most, but Matt breathed his way through like a woman in labor about to give her final push. The handle tore through his muscles and scraped against bone as he wrenched himself free and fell to the ground, thanking God.

Through the woods, as fast as his feet would take him, Matt raced. He attempted to mind his footing, keeping one hand pressed against his shoulder. Pausing for the briefest of moments, he realized in his haste to flee, he hadn't paid attention to which direction he'd taken off in. Needing a moment to orient himself, Matt stopped only to see the flash moving through the branches toward him. Panicked and unfocused, he took off without noticing the series of bulky exposed roots on the ground beneath him, which caught his foot and sent him tumbling down a small hill.

Matt didn't see where he landed, but a cold wetness smeared across his face when he connected with the ground. Leaning up, he learned what cushioned his fall—a human body. One wearing a familiar yellow shirt. The deceased Guide's stomach had been violently ripped open with his intestines fanned out on the ground in front of him.

Backing away from the dead boy, Matt desperately wiped the festering sludge from his face and found the bug-infested gore covered both of his hands as well, stretching out in slimy strings between his fingers. Turning away, ready to vomit and cry, he found another yellow shirt. This Guide laid face-first in a bear trap and what remained was a mangled, bloody, and dirt-covered mess, looking more like ground beef than a human face. Matt spun away from the sight only to find a third dead body: another Guide propped up against a tree with his head slumped to the side and a pickaxe lodged diagonally through his skull.

Matt stood on shaking feet, unable to process the gruesome scene encircling him. He readied himself to run again, but the Man appeared, stepping out of nowhere. There was no time for Matt to question the how or why. There was not even a chance to react as the rusted axe blade, still dripping with Killian's blood, planted itself deeply into the middle of Matt's smooth, handsome face.

☠

The Mercedes' tires spun wildly, kicking up the driveway's dirt and gravel as the car sped from Horizons. Tyler stood in the wake with his duffel bag at his feet and his middle finger extended up and high. Neither of them had so much as a given him a parting glance. No hugs, no goodbye waves upon their hasty departure. Part of him wanted to cry because, for him, his parents had died the minute his father handed his credit card over. Bob's greedy eyes had lit up when he slid the gold card through the reader. After the approval popped up, Michael had escorted Nadine out to the car without some much as a word to his one and only son.

When the car's engine faded into the distance, Tyler slung the duffel bag over his shoulder and followed the tire marks in the drive with no intention of remaining at Camp Horizons.

"Excuse me, young man, where exactly do you think you're going?" Bob asked, trotting down the front stairs trying to catch up to Tyler.

"Seriously?" Tyler shouted at him and, again, shot up his middle finger. "You got paid, dude. Keep the money, I'm out. I'll find a nice stranger
at the bus station to blow for a bus ticket out of here. My skills are top-notch, *vigorous* even." Tyler poked his tongue into his cheek as he made the blow job motion with his hand and laughed at how red Bob's face turned. He found brief joy in seeing the camp director flummoxed.

"*God sees you*, Tyler Wills." Bob leered at Ty as he spouted his favorite catchphrase again. He stopped and put a hand on his hip as he caught his breath and motioned toward the road. "It's forty-five miles to the bus depot, but feel free to make that hike. One call to the sheriff and you'll be back here before the end of the day. You're a minor, 'member? And all the paperwork your parents happily signed makes me your legal guardian for the next two weeks. So, in other words—"

"Yeah." Tyler already started walking back pissed and determined to find another way out. "I don't need whatever your southern country-fried version of *I'm screwed* is. I get it."

Bob smirked, appearing to feel quite righteous at his victory as he led Tyler to the main trail through Horizons known as Harmony Lane. Its name carved into the wooden post, erected in the air like a street sign and marked on each side by old, splintering railroad ties, which lined up from the driveway's circle and trailed down through the eight sleeper cabins. Harmony Lane split off to the left and right, and those trails appeared to circle through the defunct archery range and picnic areas before they met up again and followed the lake shore.

Bob rattled off the rules as they walked between the Integrity Cabin, where the primary therapy happened, and the mess hall down toward the sleeper cabins. "You are, at all times, to remain in Camp Horizons dress code. Your attire is waiting for you in the cabin, and you'll be provided with as many shirts and khaki pants as you need. We, as a cohesive unit, wash all soiled clothes every week, along with cleaning the cabins, the restrooms, the kitchen, and tending to the grounds. Service is God's bridle, and you will help clean and weed the beautiful camp he has gifted us while we clean and weed your soul.

"Your parents should have packed a selection of oversized white T-shirts and extra-large plain boxers, which are to be worn under your clothes at all times, *even* when you are sleeping. You are at no time to be semi or fully naked with another

Journeyer present."

"I don't wear underwear, restricts my fat cock." Tyler grabbed himself for added measure and laughed until Bob spun around and pointed a firm finger directly into his chest.

"Now listen up, you little smart aleck, the paperwork your parents signed gives me leeway to do *many* things, and one of them is the right to conduct a body check on you at any time to ensure your compliance." Bob lost his grandiose, holier-than-thou preacher vibe and behaved more like the tired, overworked camp director he appeared to truly be. The parents were gone, the show was over. "You are here to find your way to the Lord, and I suggest you remember that. It's time to accept your *Journey* has begun."

Tyler scoffed, cursing his parents and the group of weirdos they left him with.
What permissions and power had these assholes been granted to do to him?

Bob continued his spiel as he led Tyler to the cabin marked *A*. "You will shower one at a time and always with a Guide posted at the entrance. You will enter fully clothed, and you will exit fully dried and clothed. Both of your shirts are to remain on at all times, no matter the heat index."

"But we sleep in the same cabin?"

"Yes, and one of the Guides or myself will perform checks throughout the night. As I stated before, any inappropriate touching of oneself, or male-on-male contact, will reset your *Journey*."

"Wait, I can't jerk off? I'm seventeen, dude. I got needs. What's with your religion always feeling the need to control what people do with their own bodies? You do get it's creepy, right? God made me this horny and hung."

Bob shook his head indignantly. "You find this humorous? Everything a joke to you? This, Tyler, is real life, and you'll take this *Journey* seriously. We're here to save your filthy foul soul, so one day, you'll be able to walk alongside our Heavenly Father again. To be there with him, to bask in the love he has for all his children."

"Just not as myself, right? I can't like the feeling of another guy on top of me *and* still get in on this all-encompassing love, huh? I don't think I want to be loved by someone with that kind of ideology, *Bob*." Whenever Tyler spoke the camp director's name, he drew the word out and added as much disdain and disrespect as he could, smiling while he did.

Ty hated his parents for leaving him with this insufferable clown, but the fear that Bob or one of the other Guides would physically harm him began to grow like a leafy vine in the back of his mind. He'd defend himself if things came to it; fuck anyone who tried to lay their hands on him. But the shit still scared him.

Being seventeen was bullshit; Tyler understood how the world worked, how fucked up life treated him, and yet, legally found himself unable to do anything about the injustices being cast on him. Tyler wished more than once he'd been born a bit dimmer—less aware of the world around him—like his classmates appeared to have been. But no, to Tyler seventeen felt like twenty-five, and because of a blow job he was now trapped. The Camp Horizons logo mocked him from the shirt of a thirty-something overweight and balding stranger who'd been given complete authority over him.

"You have fallen off the path Tyler, but God loves you, nonetheless. And that's what all of this is here for. We are bringing you back to him, and things like self-gratification and physical contact with others is detrimental to the *Journey*. When they say, *'Cleanliness is next to Godliness,'* they don't mean our surroundings or our bodies; they are referring to our minds too. And Tyler, our minds are dirtier than other peoples. We must work harder. We've been tricked into believing this way of life is our intended path—it is not.

"When I came here, I was like you. I believed nothing was wrong with me. And my two weeks here proved transformative." Bob's eyes glazed over remembering the fond times as he spoke about how his tenure at Horizons changed him for the better. "I found a way to return to my Lord. And that's why I opted to take over this camp when the man who guided me through my *Journey* retired. We bring those who are lost back to our Lord. They simply need a Guide. Let me guide you, Tyler." Bob let the authority lapse from his voice, trying to be friendly and compassionate. Ty knew if there had been a chair there for him to turn around and sit backwards in during his talk, he would have. "Let me help you return to the Lord. I can guide you on the path to finding him again, Tyler. He misses you."

Tyler followed along with an obviously fake sincerity before leaning into Bob. "You get how fucking culty you sound, right?"

Bob quickly snapped out of his let-me-save-you shtick. "*Dearly beloved, I beseech you as strangers and pilgrims, abstain from fleshly lusts, which rage war against the soul.'* Stop raging war against your own soul, Mr. Wills." He pointed to the cabin to their right. "Cabin *A* is for Journeyers. The others arrived yesterday. We pushed the start of the cycle to accommodate your last-minute arrival, but tonight," he warned, "we will begin."

"Aww, for me? You shouldn't have." Ty mimicked a feminine voice and held his hands limply up at his chest. He didn't care for the stereotypical charade personally, but the act appeared to annoy Bob, which had been Ty's intention.

The camp director left him in a huff, demanding Tyler not change into his Horizons garb until a Guide named Kevin came to escort him to the showers. Tyler flicked him off, hoping he would turn around and see his extended finger. Ty enjoyed mocking Bob with this thick accent and the intense love for Jesus, but in his head, those leafy vines of fear stretched out with all the different ideas of what they might do to him.

Tyler swung the heavier-than-expected door, which slammed against the side of the cabin and marred his graceful entrance. The cabin, like a trailer, was longer than wide with a row of bunk beds running along each wall all the way to the back. At the front, a table and a ratty old couch, which Ty guessed would be more comfortable than the old bunks. On the table were three sets of tan khaki pants and three sky-blue T-shirts with the same Camp Horizons logo embossed on the front. Tyler set his duffel bag down and pulled up one of the shirts, noticing they were two sizes larger than the medium he wore.

"They don't want your body being exposed by anything form-fitting." A young person sashayed forward from the middle of the cabin, and with an Eartha Kitt growl, extended a dainty left hand forward. Tyler took their hand with his fingers and shook it gently like he had met a royal. "Jamal, and my pronouns are they, them, and *damn gurrrrrrl*, but the last one is only when I'm in drag." They spun the oversized blue shirt around like a long dress. "And yes, it is a pleasure to meet—me." Jamal laughed.

Tyler introduced himself. "Hi, I'm Tyler, my pronouns are he, him, or 'dude' is cool actually. It's nice to meet you. Bob told me to wait for Kevin before I changed?"

"Oh, the cute one. Yassss, he's got like this rough, shaved-head farmhand vibe, and I can-not. Why do conservative men always flood my basement?" Jamal gleefully dipped their own petite frame as if in the middle of an elaborate dance number while still managing to converse with Tyler. "And...you can wait for him yes, *or,* and this a better idea, you can change right here. I promise, I won't snitch." Jamal's eyes trailed down to Tyler's crotch, accompanied by a voracious tongue pop.

"I like you." Tyler found himself impressed by the twirling, dipping, nonconforming drag queen, whose makeup, they explained, had been cruelly confiscated upon arrival. "But I'm not quite ready to ignite the riot that gets us kicked out of here."

Jamal's eyes widened at the thought. "Oh yes, hunty, please. Rescue me." They sang the last words, mimicking the old song, and twirled again.

"You shouldn't be joking about that." A meek but whiney voice drifted up from the bottom bunk to Tyler's left where the sheets from the top had been pulled down to enclose the sleeping quarters.

"That's Myer, ignore her." Jamal rolled their eyes as they twisted around and faced Myer's bunk. "Ain't hurting nothin' to make a crack about this place, Myer. We're all stuck here."

The young man poked his pale, sad face out from his tent. His round metal-frame glasses made his hazel eyes look bigger than they were as he examined Tyler. "My *Journey* will not be compromised. That's why I have the sheets. And I ask you to respect that." His voice raised on the last words, suggesting the others had not been so keen to do so. "It's nice to meet you. Now leave me alone."

Tyler nodded, having no reason to disagree. "Sure dude, whatever gets you off."

"And do not change in here," Myer requested sternly, looking at Jamal and then up at the top bunk across from him, where the fourth Journeyer slept with his bare leg hanging off the side, before he ducked behind the sheeted fortress where he could be heard mumbling prayers.

"Sleeping beauty up there is Chris." Jamal shook the post of the bunk, and the thick-built football player popped up with one eye still closed and his brown curly hair a mess. He stretched his muscular arms out, which pushed out his bare barrel chest, glistening from the midday heat. "Girl, we have company."

Chris jumped down, wearing nothing but a pair of loose boxers that did nothing to hide the swinging bat between his legs. "Hey, new guy, we've been waiting for you. I'm Chris. Not quite sure if I'm a fag or not, but here I am." Behind him, Jamal danced around to the other side and peered over at Tyler, mouthing the words, *yes, he is.*

Tyler winced. "Got to be honest, Chris. I don't care much for the *F* word."

The jock's almond-shaped eyes were diverted off into the air, most likely trying to determine in his head what Tyler meant before the realization dawned on him. "Oh, sorry. Been trying to not say that word since all this went down. Kind of still figuring things out, ya know."

"Yes, I do." If they had walked past each other in the halls at school, Chris probably would have been the one to call Tyler a homo. And Tyler would have been instantly attracted to him as that's
how shit worked in his brain. But at Horizons, the handsome football player was both scared and uncertain about a future which no longer made sense. "So, your parents ditched you all here too?" Tyler asked, throwing his duffel bag on a bunk next to where the other three had gotten situated.

Jamal rolled their eyes as they all shook their heads. "My father is a big ol' Atlanta defense lawyer. And honey, Southern black lawyers do not have prancing divas for a child, especially an up and coming drag queen with an Instagram following for days. But that is according to his own ignorant ass. And thus, I got sent here to be the *sole* unicorn of color in this, the whitest of white places imaginable, and trust a girl ain't happy about it. And yet, with no gowns, no makeup, and no patience for the great outdoors, she still here, and still fucking fabulous."

"My parents caught me with my friend,"

Chris added. "Well, he wasn't actually a friend. He tutored me, and I don't know how, but things started happening, and he ended up blowing me, and that's when my parents walked in. They freaked out." Chris still seemed dazed from the speed of which the events in his life occurred, nearly as fast as Tyler's own situation. "Everything since has been a blur."

Tyler couldn't help but feel sorry for him. It was one thing to know who you were and be sent to a place like Horizons. But to be confused, as most young queer people were, and then forced to listen to the shit people like Bob spewed from their ignorant mouths was another.

"I requested to come here," Myer proclaimed proudly. His voice floated out from behind the sheets, but he did not make an appearance. "I'm sick, and this is where I need to be so I can heal."

"Doesn't look like there is anything wrong with you to me." Tyler unpacked his bag, removing the packages of new oversized white T-shirts and boxers.

"I'm gay." Myer spoke the words with the same stern seriousness often reserved for talking about a stage-four cancer patient's chances.

"Is that all?" Tyler dismissed Myer's perceived condition as he tossed his underclothes on the bed, wondering where he would be putting them until he found a trundle drawer under his bunk.

"It's a legitimate illness," Myer defended from behind his tent. "This is not what God intended for you or me."

"Well not a sickness," Tyler corrected. "And there is nothing wrong with you, me, or the equally fabulous Jamal and Chris over there. Not to get all pop power anthem on your ass, but we *were* born this way, so don't let some bigots Jedi mind-trick you into hating yourself."

"I hate the sickness, not myself." His tiny voice grew more defensive. "I hate a world that focuses on sex." Myer slid out of the bunk and stood up in the middle of the aisle, staring at Tyler, holding his Bible against his chest as tightly as he could as if it were his holy armor. "I *am* sick. I am here to get better. The Bible says—"

"I don't give a damn what the book says. I'm tired of the Bible being thrown in my face as someone's justification to treat other people like shit." Tyler kicked his trundle drawer under the bed as Myer huffed loudly before pushing his way past them and out of the cabin.

"Honey, that boy is the Super Bowl of self-abuse. Girl needs some love...and dick." Jamal cackled and playfully batted Chris's arm. "Butch, why don't you throw her a home run or whatever sports term works in this situation. Goal, maybe?" Jamal flashed a toothy smile at Chris, as he grimaced and fervently shook his head.

Tyler didn't hear any of the exchange; his hands found the only nonclothing, nonpersonal hygiene item in the bag—a letter with "Tyler, Love Mom" scribbled across the front. His fingers traced over her writing, following along her impressive cursive loops before crumpling the letter in his hands. He didn't need to know what that woman thought now. His back to the others, he allowed the tears to well up—not that he cared if anyone saw his watery eyes. His mother hurt him. The deepest betrayal from the one person supposed to love and protect him over all others. Instead, she signed his rights away and left without a word, and a few pages of pretty cursive apologies were not about to explain away what she'd done.

"Do they honestly try to fix you here?" Tyler shoved the crumpled note into the bag and stuffed the flattened duffel under the bed.

"Oh yes, these Bible-thumping Saltines are ser-i-ous, girl." Jamal spread out across their bunk, basking in a luxurious surrounding only they could see. "Since you weren't here yet, we prayed. All damn day. Myer was in heaven. But ain't no one fixin' anything honey. Many have tried, baby. Many. Have. Tried. I've simply proven too fierce to fix."

"Saltines?" Tyler questioned.

"Crackers, girl." Jamal then clarified as if Tyler should have known. "Crackers."

The cabin door swung open unexpectedly as the Guide, Kevin, stormed in, ready to catch someone in the act of something. Tyler would learn that was how Guides entered every room at Horizons. Chris had already put his uniform on, another reason for Tyler to be pissed at Nadine; her letter cost him seeing the cutie Chris shirtless one final time.

"Tyler, let's go." Kevin was as attractive as Jamal suggested, and Tyler swooned momentarily at the rough and rugged country boy until remembering who the goon worked for. Grabbing his Horizons uniform off the table, he checked out the Guide's ass as he followed Kevin out the door, giving a wink and a nod to Jamal as he passed.

☠

Bob's left hand held his lower jaw as his fingers softly massaged the soreness. The thick Southern drawl put on for the Wills, for all the parents who brought their children to Horizons, was phony. His real country twang was much tamer, but Northerners loved them an amped up accent. And it got results. Bob believed the thicker the accent, the closer to God. *Those Southerners are so much more devout.* Most of the troubled youth brought to Horizons came from Northern states, and that fact alone confirmed his theory. So, he didn't mind putting on the show and getting the occasional bout of lockjaw from servicing his Lord.

Tyler Wills would be an issue, and his *Journey* would be challenging to navigate. Thankfully, Bob had skilled Guides this cycle—too many for so few Journeyers. There were only four; the lowest the camp's attendance had dipped so far. Bob blamed the number of states passing measures to ban conversion therapy, which brought a spotlight on the conversion centers and forced a more vocal public discussion. When Bob came to Horizons in his youth, conversions centers were places spoken about discreetly and never by their name. *Oh, Bobby? Well, he's at his grandmother's,* the same cover story used for his multiple trips to the camp.

Those days of quiet visibility were gone, and Horizons' reputation was sliding fast. The camp had turned into a dumping-off point for queer troubled youths. Parents wouldn't care if their child healed or not; they wanted the queer offender out of the way.

If they came back aligned with the Lord, great. If their *Journey* needed to be extended longer, hell, no problem. Here's another check to the cover the trouble. At worst, if the Journeyer ran away, the response would always be a quiet and curt "thank you for trying," and then a dial tone. No one ever inquired about the runaways.

Bob hadn't been prepared for how. He had been successful in the program and returned the administrative side of the center worked every couple of years as a Guide to help others. Those experiences were beautiful, soul-filling, and uplifting, but being camp director proved harder than he expected.

"I've not seen Killian *or* Matt since this morning when they went on a walk," Lisa announced as she walked in, taking a seat at the desk to the left with an exasperated sigh as if their disappearance created more work for her. "A *walk*, sure." She banged the folders on the desk signaling she was there.

Every decision and every step he made which had led to Bob sitting at the "big desk," as they called the monstrosity, were divinely inspired. The night he'd been feeling weak, his spirit slipping, he almost made a mistake. Instead, he reached out to his old Guide and mentor, Chester Barrett. The retiring camp director was friendly and caring, and shortly after their reconnection, Bob agreed to take over as Horizon's new director.

He all but moved to the camp and spent nearly a year shadowing Chester before the retiring director handed Bob the keyring and left. The new position, the new challenge, renewed his passion in life. And that excitement was invigorated with every interview conducted for what would be his own set of Guides. Once all his applicants had spoken the exact words Bob wanted to hear, he believed he'd found the absolute perfect crew to help bring Horizons back to its former glory.

Divinely inspired, yes, but Bob quickly found out the truth; attendance dropped and had not bounced back, the financials were bleak, and all that occurred before Chester left. After he did, the decline grew worse. Bob lost three of his perfectly picked Guides, who walked off the job without a single word.

The annoying Lisa was one of the backups. Not having gone through conversion therapy herself, Bob had reluctantly hired her. When he requested a second interview to create a list of alternates, she explained her desire to help other lost souls stemmed from her brother, who had gone through the *Journey* but taken his life a couple years after graduating from the camp.

She couldn't help him, but she was determined to help others. After his third Guide ran off, he called and asked her to come help.

A regrettable decision. whether a male or female Guide, there was a certain character needed by all to handle the job at hand. Bob did not believe Lisa possessed such character and found many of her personality traits, such as her boorish attitude, extremely annoying in the week and a half she'd been there. Her goal appeared to be trying to find Guides and Journeyers slipping for the sole purpose of getting to be the one to call them out. An attitude which did not sit well with Bob, but he needed the help for the moment. After this cycle, she, Matt, and Craig—the only other Guide in his late thirties—would all have to be let go. Bob knew the place would run with his three *K*'s: Kevin, Killian, and Karen, his friend and the camp's cook. The idea of having to let anyone go hurt his heart.

"How long have they been gone?" He did not want to indulge her, but curiosity propelled him to do so.

"*Hours.*" Lisa exaggerated the word in a sing-song voice, insinuating something more salacious transpired.

"All right, but how many? Like, long enough there may have been an accident, and we should be worried?"

"A few." She corrected her tone to one more concerning.

Bob wished she'd said, "only a couple" since a "few" didn't sit well with him. "Well, I'm sure there is a solid reason for their absence, and we will learn all about it when they get back. First Night begins soon, and they know they're needed."

Lisa perked up. She had missed the start of the last cycle and now repeatedly hounded Bob to witness the First Night and sit in. She claimed the act would make her feel closer to her brother.

He sensed her gearing up to ask again and stopped her. "Which again, Lisa, is only for those who have been through the *Journey* and those starting." While he appreciated her enthusiasm, a little went a long way. "Is Karen set in the kitchen?"

"Yes." The response came flying at him hot and snooty. "The menu's adjusted to accommodate the lower attendance. Is patronage always this low?"

Her endless inquisitiveness was another trait Bob found extremely annoying, along with the constant references she made to her brother's suicide. "The number of Journeyers is not relevant. Only that the ones present are given our full attention when starting their *Journey*." She agreed and flipped through her folders as if returning to work, which confused Bob since the Guides were not given paperwork to contend with. But he didn't question things, opting to ignore her instead.

"That forking kid," Kevin yelled, barging into the office cursing under his breath, hands balled tightly, and his body shaking. He drew his breath in and exhaled loudly. "Lord, forgive me and grant me strength." He closed his eyes and stood silently in prayer until sitting down, then threw his feet up on the desk, pinched the bridge of his nose with his fingers, and withheld the string of vulgarity he wished to spew forth knowing it would be unacceptable spoken aloud. "It was a simple request to change his clothes, and he turned the whole thing into a debate over basic human rights."

"*Fathers, do not exasperate your children; instead, bring them up in the training and the instruction of our Lord.*" Bob stayed ready with verses, which he whipped out for any situation. "He will be a challenge, and we will be all that more successful when we return such a deeply troubled soul to the Lord."

"I don't know. I kind of want to throttle him." Kevin punched his palm and took another deep breath.

"Is he that bad?" Lisa bounced in her seat, excited for a bit of drama to spice up her day.

Bob cleared his throat loudly and bowed his head. *"If any of you lacks wisdom, you should ask God, who gives generously to all without finding fault, and it will be given to you. But when you ask, you must believe and not doubt because the one who doubts is like a wave of the sea, blown and tossed by the wind. That person should not expect to receive anything from the Lord."* He opened his eyes and looked at them as if the quote alone needed no further explanation.

"Now, instead of shining lights on his faults or the undoubted nuisance he is sure to be, we must do as scripture states in James and remain strong in our faith and ask our Lord to guide us. If the Journey were easy, they wouldn't need us. Remember that."

Bob raised a solitary finger in the air and spoke with the utmost seriousness. "Only we can guide these lost souls back to God. I would like everyone to spend extra time down on their knees before we begin tonight and don't get up until you're sure God has come—to you with the strength you'll need to guide our charges."

☠

Tyler trailed behind the Guide, Craig, who'd come to collect the Journeyers once the sun set and bring them to their First Night, as he called the event. Tyler walked up the path, feeling silly in his oversized shirt, which billowed on his lean frame like a flowy blouse, and the khakis, which he pulled the belt around to the very last hole to get to stay up. The clothing was a necessity to desexualize the

Journeyers and limit temptation, or so Kevin had explained to Tyler when he went to the restroom to change. Ty replied that he should have been provided with a matching ski mask as well since it was his face, not his body, that the guys wanted to come all over. Unsurprisingly, he found Kevin did not care for such brazen vulgarity, but Ty laughed his ass off anyway as he went in to change.

No one was laughing now. The four Journeyers followed Craig around to the front of Integrity Cabin. He told them to wait at the end of the walkway as Bob and Kevin stepped down from the porch and approached them.

Bob's voice echoed out over the quiet camp boisterously, as if he addressed a thousand young men readying for war. "Tonight, you begin your *Journey* from a life of perverse sexual brokenness to one of undeniable and perpetual happiness. You are not starting a new path; you are returning to the one you've been led astray from. The path that leads you directly to our Lord almighty. There is truthfully no better place to be. And if you young men were forthright and honest with yourselves"—he made eye contact with each of them as he spoke—"you would freely admit how unhappy in your own skin you truly are. You will find that these feelings are not authentic to your soul. They are not what God wants for you. Boys, once you accept that, the Journey will be easier for you." He stepped in front of Jamal and stared directly into their eyes for a silent minute before asking, "Why are you here?"

Jamal glanced around the camp, looking to the others, confused at the question. Bob impatiently tapped his foot, repeating the question, unrelenting until Jamal gave him an answer. "I'm here...to be straight as fuck, hunty. Didn't you know that already Boo?"

Bob scowled, his round face scrunching in disgust, but motioned for Jamal to move past and enter the cabin He faced Myer next, repeating the question. Myer's gaze remained where it had the whole day, down at his feet, as he mumbled his sheepish answer about wanting to be cured. His earned him a warm acknowledgement from Bob, who waved him on and moved in front of Tyler. "And Mr. Wills, why are you here?"

"Your shithole camp popped up first on my father's Google search."

"You can fight this." Bob sneered, leaning into him. "It's only going to make the *Journey* harder for you. You're sick, Tyler," he insisted before waving him through.

Bob repeated the question again to Chris, who replied he didn't know. And Tyler couldn't help but hear the honesty in his answer and feel the ache growing within his heart. Tyler feared Bob would fuck Chris's head up more so than it had already been. As he walked up the stairs, both Kevin and Craig eyed him cautiously. Tyler wanted to flick them off, blow them a kiss, or worse, but the only option was to play somewhat nice.

Integrity Cabin was little more than a rec hall. Along its front wall were a kitchenette, an empty pantry, and a counter with some stools. Most of the space was vacant and open with a raised platform positioned against the center of the back wall, above which hung a crucifix. Tyler walked toward the four chairs seated in front of the stage and passed multiple racks holding over a hundred more dust-covered plastic folding chairs. The room fit a hundred and fifty people comfortably, and Tyler wondered about the times when the cabin reached such capacity. With only seven of them in there, the cabin seemed more like a grand empty ballroom, expect Tyler assumed—and correctly—there'd be no dancing.

The four Journeyers sat in their seats and faced the giant cross with Bob appearing small as he paced the stage, mumbling prayers to himself. Nothing about the cabin made Tyler feel comfortable for the vibe within the room was highly oppressive. When he glanced over his shoulder, Craig bolted the cabin's three heavy-duty locks. There was only one small window in the entire space too, over the kitchenette's sink where Kevin stood with arms folded, stone-faced, and quiet like a Christian thug.

Bob's prayers ended, and the echo of his voice bounced off the walls in the empty cabin around them. "Homosexuality is an affliction. A disease. And despite what the media would have you believe it is not another facet of everyday life. No. Homosexuality is a condition. And one that can be reversed. You can be capable of leading happy heterosexual lives, secure in the knowledge God loves you, and you will have a place in his kingdom when this world ends. He wants you to be the heterosexual you were born to be. This noisy world, with its loud, repetitive music and suggestive television programs, has poisoned your minds. They've made you believe that relationships with other men are acceptable. *They are not*", he bellowed. "There is no future in homosexual relationships, not in this world, and certainly not within the kingdom of heaven. It is disgusting to lie with another man. And your souls are filthy for the mere thought of engaging in these acts, and for allowing depraved thoughts to dwell within your hearts and minds.

We will clear this sickness from you, for we have succeeded cleansing this sickness from from ourselves. Amen."

"I know how all of you think." Bob lowered his voice, retaining his pompous and proud tone as if a dozen TV cameras were fixed on him. "I know how you act, especially when no one is looking. I know what's hidden on your phones and what spurs lust in your hearts. You have no secrets from me. Or from Him." Bob's pointer finger raised up to the sky. "*God sees you.* Everything you do. Everything you think and feel. It's time for you to see how your affliction is making you sicker." Bob shifted to the dramatic, getting louder and putting on an excellent show to ensure God stopped his daily routine to pay attention.

"You cannot function out in the world as an average, God-fearing man with this perversion weighing you down. Accept you are disgusting. Accept you have foul hearts and diseased minds. And let God's word heal you: '*Let us examine and probe our ways and let us return to the Lord.*' And examining your ways is what we will be doing over the next two weeks—perhaps longer for some." Bob narrowed his eyes and directed his pointed glance at Tyler, who rolled his eyes in response. "God never wanted you to be queer—never. Queerness is not his creation. It's an abomination," he shouted, "plain and simple. And our Lord does not want you defiling the bodies He gifted you with by engaging in these filthy, unnatural acts. They are—"

"Well documented," Tyler interrupted, not caring he wasn't supposed to talk, nor caring about the repercussions, which almost never occurred to him anyway. "Homosexual behavior is recorded in over 1,500 animal species. It's considered by most scientists to be completely natural. Are you trying to tell me that penguins are disgusting, foul-souled creatures as well? Wait, that's right, you don't believe animals have souls, do you?" Tyler shook his head at the ridiculous notion, which any loving pet owner would happily debunk.

"We are speaking about human beings and their errant behaviors, not animals. I will appreciate you do not interrupt me again," Bob snapped.

"Did God not create penguins? It's a simple question, *Bob*." Tyler tried not to miss any opening there was to skewer the camp director's name.

"Tyler, this is not a forum for discussion."

"Did God not create lions? The other day, I watched this video of two male lions like, going at it, and I'm tellin' you, they seemed hella natural to me. Is the king of the jungle a foul-souled creature as well?"

Jamal let a squeal of delight slip from their lips, but instantly covered their mouth.

Tyler's focus remained on Bob's face, but in his peripheral vision, he caught a glimpse of Kevin and Craig inching closer to the group, positioning themselves behind his chair.

"Every homosexual relationship is sinful," Bob scolded. *"Man shall not lie with man, as he does with a woman.'* That is God's word, from the good book itself. How dare you question it?"

Tyler laughed, openly and loudly, giving no fucks. "And I believe your 'good book' also states in Leviticus that men will not shave their faces or their heads." Tyler glanced over his shoulder, noticing the other two Guides had moved a little closer, as he motioned to Craig's smooth face and Kevin's shaved head. *"And the swine, though he divide the hoof, and be cloven-footed, yet he cheweth not the curd; HE is unclean to you."* What exactly did we have for dinner, Bob? I do believe there was ham in that there soup."

"I got fed unclean swine?" Jamal exclaimed dramatically. "I did not consent to that. No ma'am. No sir. Save my soul Black Jesus." Jamal fanned themself as if they were in their Georgia church on a hot Sunday afternoon.

"Wait, no bacon?" Chris asked, turning to Tyler. "No chops? Why not?"

Bob's angry face glared down at Jamal and Chris, who quieted themselves. Myer remained in his seat, faced forward, appearing pissed at the interruption.

"There is a whole list of shit we can't eat, can't touch, can't do. But we aren't following that to the letter now are we, Bob?"

Frustrated, but doing his best to hide it, Bob paced the stage and spewed more Bible verses. *"In the same way the men also abandoned natural relations with women and were inflamed with lust for one another. Men committed shameful acts with* other men and received in themselves the due penalty for their error.' It's written in more than one section of the Bible. There are multiple verses related to your depravity, Tyler. God does not want this for you. This is not in his divine plan."

"*For it was you who formed my inward parts; you knit me together in my mother's womb. I praise you, for I am fearfully and wonderfully made.'* I know the Bible too, you charlatan." Tyler sat up taller in his seat ready to match Bob Bible verse to Bible verse. "He made me, didn't he? Like he made those penguins and boss-ass lions." Bob appeared flustered, his face growing redder with every exchange, and Ty enjoyed the torment he dished out. "*Beloved, let us love one another, because love is from God; everyone who loves is born of God and knows God.'* What I don't get, Bob, is there are some 30,000 verses in that Bible of yours, yet only six of them reference queer people. Two thousand of them are about greed; tell me, how much did you charge my parents for this bullshit? You don't get to pick the parts that serve your agenda and ignore the rest, asshole."

Bob motioned with his head, and Kevin and Craig sprung forward and grabbed Tyler by the shoulders before yanking him from the chair.

"Get you fucking hands off me." Tyler kicked at the air, yelling as they moved him, and knocked the chair over, which crashed loudly on the floor in the near-empty room.

"Take him to the Hut," Bob ordered, smiling as the Guides dragged Tyler toward the door. "He can spend the night out there until he calms down."

"You're a piece of shit," Tyler screeched.

"There is nothing wrong with any of us." Kevin sent his free hand across Ty's face with a hard slap. He winced with pain but continued undeterred.

Tyler yelled, directing each fiery word at Bob. *"Not everyone who says to me, Lord, will enter the kingdom of Heaven."* Kevin sent his fist into Tyler's stomach, but the violent act did not stop the young man. *"On that day many will say, Lord, did we not prophesy in your name? Cast out demons in your name? Do mighty works in your name?"* Tyler's voice carried as they removed him from Integrity Cabin. His final words sliding in right before the door slammed closed. *"And I will declare to them—I never knew you."*

☠

In the mess hall, Lisa sat at the island in the kitchen, enjoying a soda and reading her Bible as Karen—once a Journeyer herself—finished drying the pots from dinner. The women glanced at each other when Tyler's shouting, as they dragged him across the camp, shook them out of the silence they'd been sitting in. His voice rang out again, calling Kevin and Craig a variety of names and insults, and all went quiet after they hit him several more times.

"First Night can be rough." Karen shook her head and set the last large pot on the counter to dry. "He ain't gonna like the Hut." Sitting at the island across from Lisa, Karen slid her dinner in front of her. She didn't like to eat until after everything had been done. That way, as she explained to Lisa, she could sit peacefully and enjoy. Only Bob ate after her and she didn't mind cleaning up after him.

"What's the Hut?" Lisa asked curiously, perking up in her seat.

"It's a time-out shack in the woods. He'll be spending the night there most likely." Karen ate the ham and bean soup she had made for their supper and flipped through an old *People* magazine while trying to avoid looking at Lisa's buxom chest in her yellow shirt. "Not really a pleasant place to be."

"Have you ever spent the night out there?"

Karen went quiet. She didn't care to discuss the three nights she spent in there after telling them where to shove their holy book. It was the past, and she preferred to remain in the present. Across the counter, she could see the questions bubbling up inside the perky young Guide, and thought of ways of deflecting. "No, I've never been there, but I know it's awful."

"Oh." Lisa pouted, unhappy with the answer, and let her focus drift across the room until returning to Karen's unsmiling face. "Well, how was your First Night then? I'm really interested." She leaned forward like they were a couple girlfriends at brunch, hoping Karen would spill all the tea over their Bloody Mary's.

Clearing her throat, Karen shifted in her seat. "It's intense, and that's all I'd like to say about it. Our *Journey* is a private matter." She shoveled another spoonful of her dinner, the one she wanted to sit down and enjoy alone.

Lisa rolled her eyes. Sighing, and bored of her surroundings, she fidgeted in her chair, pressing her chest out as she extended her arms in a wide stretch. Karen tried hard to not notice them, but the Guide's ample breasts were blatantly on display. "I'm so curious about the whole process, is all. I wish they'd let me in."

"It is only for those on their *Journey,* which Bob has explained to you."

"I know." Her words came out like a whiney teenage girl, which frustrated Karen. "My goal is to help all the queer boys of this world. My brother was gay, you know, and I loved him so much. But then he took his own life, and you know?"

"Yes, I do know," Karen added sardonically. "You've mentioned that fact more than a few times now." Lisa brought up her dead brother as often as possible. Karen attempted to keep her eyes on the *People* magazine, not reading any of the words written as her gaze continued to drift back across the island to Lisa's chest.

"I have a lot to learn, but I'm up for the challenge. I know I have to work harder, not being an ex-gay and all, but the Lord said to me, Lisa Marie, this is your callin' darlin'. Help them simple queer fools. This was after, you know, my brother took his life. So, I said, yes, God, I *am* up for the challenge. I'm going to make sure all those homos get in correct with the Lord. And I have a secret weapon too." Lisa whispered as she cupped her chest and gave her girls a firm shake up and down, "Those boys need a peek at some of the goods God has waiting for them once they get straightened out. My girls here will keep them motivated to come to Jesus—instead of coming in each other."

"Sounds like a good motivator." Karen struggled not to dwell on Lisa's prominently displayed chest.

Lisa bounced in her chair, flashing brightly

with delight. "Everything I do...I do for the Lord. See this?" She pulled down the neck of her T-shirt and pulled up a crucifix on a long chain from out of her cleavage. "I keep it on me at all times. It's a reminder of what I'm here to do." She showed off the simple silver cross, letting the chain gleam in the light. Karen focused on the tiny Jesus fish painted onto Lisa's fingernails and not the deep valley of cleavage calling to her like a siren's song.

"My grandmother's, she wanted to be buried with it, *but* how do you let something so precious go into the ground? I mean, I couldn't."

"How'd you get the necklace then?" Karen asked, finding herself genuinely interested and enamored by the view.

"I snatched it off her body the day of the funeral when no one was looking." Lisa sighed softly, remembering the day and how happy she'd been with her deed. "If she lived long enough to see my brother take his own life, I believe—truly—she would've insisted I keep the chain." Lisa tucked the necklace into her T-shirt and settled into the chair. "I know I need to be more patient, but I'm ready to help these bum bandits get down with the only guy they're going to be dropping to their knees for from now on, Jesus."

Neither of the women detected the shadowed face watching them from the window, getting angrier with every beat of their conversation he overheard. An anger still burning hot from what he'd seen peeking in through the window of Integrity cabin. The hulking figure in the hoodie balled his fist and marched across the camp. With everyone occupied, nothing stopped him as he ripped the lock off the door to the utility shed and grabbed a few of the contents.

☠

Screaming carried on the wind, the primal kind, and Ty bet the noise came from the direction of Integrity Cabin. The screaming became the only thing audible as he moved around the Hut, which was slightly larger than a bathroom stall and lit by a single bulb that hung above him. Kevin and Craig literally threw him into the shack, bolted the door, and left without a word. Tyler kicked at the door, demanding they go fuck themselves, until his throat went hoarse.

Besides the echo of primal screams, the camp appeared quiet outside of the typical forest ambiance: the sawing legs of crickets, the occasional hoot of an owl or a loon, and the scurrying of small creatures in the bushes all around the Hut. Tyler peered through the cracks between the boards, trying to determine where he was, and what those lights were he saw the faint glint of off in the distance. Tyler, busy fighting against Craig and Kevin and getting hit in his sides which were now sore, didn't see which direction they'd dragged him.

"Stupid fucking religious bigots." He screamed the words with every ounce of hate he had and slammed a hand against the barred door, cupping it in his other hand when the stinging started. Turning around, he examined the interior of the tiny four-by-five-foot enclosure. The floor was dirt, and on the right side, he found his toilet, a crudely scooped out hole above which a half-used roll of toilet paper hung off a nail jutting out from the Hut's shoddy construction.

They'd provided an old, damp pillow reeking of mildew, and a blanket smelling of piss. Tyler scolded himself. Angered he hadn't played along, hadn't been quiet and simply dealt with the two weeks with a giant phony smile. He couldn't, no matter how hard he tried. More so, he wouldn't. The stubborn part of his personality ran deeper than the Mariana Trench. He might not have had the firmest of moral compasses, but what went down at Horizons was utter bullshit.

He sat against the wall and curled up with the soiled pillow between him and the dirt floor while thinking of ways to escape. Breaking out of the tiny shack proved fruitless, and he knew someone would undoubtedly collect him on the long walk to town. His oversized attire and the light blue T-shirt with the Horizons logo embossed in bright yellow on the front were huge giveaways. Some Good Samaritan would scoop him up and deliver him right back to Bob.

Though he hated the idea, he resigned himself to playing along, although he had serious doubt he could. The minute the door opened, all he wanted to do was leap out, swinging hard and fast with his queer fists of fury until their faces were bloodied, unrecognizable messes. "I bet you all love to get fisted," he yelled, despite knowing no one was around to hear.

The unmistakable noise of feet trudging through the leaves and the snapping of branches scattered on the ground around the Hut forced Tyler to sit up. "Hello?"

☠

Lisa left the kitchen and walked to the Guide's cabin where they all had their own rooms, collected her toiletries, and made her way to the ladies' restroom. She stopped more than once along her route. First to enjoy the cool five-degree drop in the temperature since the temps had been in the high nineties all week, and she welcomed the sudden break. The second, when the primal screaming therapy from the Integrity Cabin abruptly ended, startling her. The last, when she stepped along Harmony Lane on her way to cross over to the showers. Unsure of what caused the sudden chills running up and down her body, she became convinced somebody was around her—watching. Nervously, Lisa quickened her pace and rushed to the restroom. Closing the door behind her, she hovered over the lock for a moment before deciding she had been silly. No one would be out there unless Karen planned on jumping in the shower with her, which wouldn't be a surprise after the way the cook stared at her chest all evening.

Lisa moved down the row of seven dingy sinks and their accompanying mirrors and stopped at the last one before the opening to the shower stalls. Out of the seven lamps hanging down from the ceiling above her, only three of them had working bulbs. They were not bright enough to break the heavy shadows covering most of the restroom, but luckily, one of those bulbs hung over the last sink, and one worked over the shower stall she had come to prefer as well. She emptied her toiletry bag of the usual suspects; bodywash, shampoo, and conditioner, all in their own color-coordinated travel bottles, a shower puff to wash, her toothpaste and toothbrush, and a digital voice recorder.

She took cautious glances around to make sure she was alone. Showering became the only time she found any real privacy while at the camp. Even their room in the Guide's cabin provided no seclusion; there were only beaded curtains in the doorways. Bringing the recorder to her lips, she pressed the button with the red circle and checked her face and hair as she spoke. The wilderness and the heat were a bad combination for her delicate skin.

"Day eight; my undercover investigation of Camp Horizons and the alleged abuses that have occurred here since the eighties is hitting serious roadblocks. My cover, thankfully, has remained intact thus far, but it's harder than I thought to answer to a fake name all damn day." Her voice lost the constant virginal, cheery Southern bubbliness she'd spoken with since being first interviewed by Bob. "Lisa" went away for the next hour, and she could freely be herself, Erin Klein, investigative journalist.

"Tonight, a new group of young men started their Journey, as this process is referred to. They were a small group, only four, and I'll need to amp-up my attempts to uncover what these so-called 'therapeutic techniques' are by the end of this cycle. There's no word yet on another group coming in after these two weeks are over, and this may be my only shot at getting any info. If they're going under, and possibly closing, what they've done here needs to be revealed.

"Again, I found myself unable to secure a place within Integrity Cabin tonight to witness what they refer to as 'First Night,' but I've been told the experience is very intense. The way the evening has loosely been described to me made things sound as if the goal is to break the Journeyers down until they believe they are nothing. None of the staff, no matter how much I cozy up to them or befriend them, are willing to share any actual details of the Journey with me, despite the fact I was hired by the director to assist these young men and women through this experience. It doesn't make any sense why they won't let me be a part of the process.

"Camp Director Bob Kendall is a real piece of work, a liar and fraud. Boy, does he put on a show for these parents, literally says anything to get them to sign over a check. A check they're giving over so their children can be tortured. I can't determine who is worse in this situation." Erin chided herself for allowing personal feelings to creep into her notes. If she wanted to properly expose Camp Horizons' abuses, her reporting needed to be thoroughly and unbiasedly researched. And most importantly, there needed to be proof.

Lisa, the real one, was Erin's best friend since college, and her brother went through the camp's therapy only to end his own life shortly after coming home. The real Lisa hadn't pressed Erin to investigate but did not discourage her when the reporter couldn't shake off how wrong the situation felt to her. There'd been no closure for Lisa's family even two years later, and Erin believed the family deserved some. Exposing Horizons would help their grief, provide some closure, and give a boost to her career at the same time.

"The boys might be my one hope. I heard one of them being reprimanded harshly tonight, so maybe him first. If he has an issue here, maybe he'll help and give me exactly what I need: a valid first-hand account. Bob took me aside after the parents left and told me the Journeyers wouldn't have homes to return to if we are not successful in bringing them to Christ. Side note before I forget: Bob keeps all the records of past Journeyers in the bottom left drawer of his desk." Erin clicked the recorder off as she thought about the drawer with its easily pickable lock.

The story was important, too much so to put all her trust in Tyler. In those records were the names of the former Journeyers, some of whom were possibly ready to talk. The thought of what Bob would do if he found out about her ruse bothered her. The atmosphere of the camp had been tense since she arrived, and grew tenser with every cycle. And some of the off-hand comments Bob and the other Guides made led her to feel as if physical force was never entirely off the table at Horizons. After stripping off her Guide's uniform and wrapping a towel around her, Erin clicked the recorder on again.

"Second side note: I will try to get a copy of the release the parents' sign. I'm fairly certain they are unknowingly relinquishing their rights. I will have to investigate further and see if this is legal? I believe they would need a notary for something of that degree? Are the parents aware of what they're signing, or do they simply not care?" She pressed Stop, the last comment sticking with her.

How could people leave their kids in this place? She tucked the recorder back into the bag and left it sitting unevenly on the edge of the sink. Erin stopped and leaned into the mirror, taking a closer look at the blotchy redness on her face. She grabbed her toothbrush and avoided looking at her skin as she tended to her teeth; the night's dinner had left a foul taste in her mouth.

Erin was unaware, as she brushed and played with her hair in the mirror, that the door to the rest--room had opened and closed silently as someone slid in and watched her from the concealing shadows.

☠

Craig rounded up the three remaining Journeyers and escorted them from Integrity Cabin to their own. Bob lorded over them from the porch, watching them make their way down the walkway as they sobbed quietly, broken. He relished joyfully the fact he'd brought them one step closer to God.

"You've expunged the anger," he called out before they left earshot. "The anger a life of homosexuality has built up inside of you has made you sick. But tonight, you've begun to break free from that diseased way of thinking, and you are releasing the homosexuality back to the depths of hell where the foulness comes from. You should all be proud of yourselves.

"As you lay in your bunks tonight, I want you to thank merciful God in heaven for this second chance you've been given. Ask him for the courage and the strength you will need to continue the path toward salvation now you've taken the first steps of a long journey—your *Journey*. Sleep well, and may God bless all of you."

The trio did not speak but pressed on, heads lowered, eyes red and puffy, and their faces sullen as Craig walked them to their cabin.

"I'd say we pulled off a decent First Night." Kevin kept an eye on the Journeyers as they left. "Well except for one hiccup. That boy is something else. Never heard one of them throwing verses back at you like that before. What a punk." Kevin wanted to call Ty something else but left the description at punk.

"Kevin, please. He is lost in his life at this moment. And his limited knowledge of the Bible doesn't matter." Bob waved Tyler's outburst away like the verbal smackdown were nothing more than an annoying insect. "Doesn't change anything. A night in the Hut will show him his errors. Kevin, when God sends you a wild horse, you must break him till he is tame enough to ride. It's simple. When you and I came here to heal our own brokenness, we did so voluntarily, like with Myer. We had the drive to better ourselves and get back to our Lord. Myer will follow this *Journey* until the end, and he will come through the other side for he was strong enough to hear God to begin with. But when God drops them on your doorstep at the last moment, under tense circumstances, and they're too far gone to see what you're doing is for their benefit, then there is simply no other choice but to break them." The tiniest hint of malice rose in his tone.

"Have you ever handled someone like Tyler, or that effeminate one, Jamal, before?"

Bob shook his head. "As a Guide no, but ones like him pop up now and then, like in '95, but I'd rather not get into that mess." Bob immediately shut the topic down, unwilling to revisit the unpleasant memory from when he'd been there. Rehashing the woes of a tumultuous year did nothing to aid them in the present. He thanked Kevin for a good First Night before excusing himself.

☠

Erin pulled the tattered liner passing as a shower curtain aside and grumbled at the cheap plywood walls and exposed pipes which constituted her shower. After stepping in, she turned the knob and jumped back out as the nozzle began to spurt. The water would be ice cold at first, needing time to warm up, but it never got hot enough to wash off the filth of the camp and the woods.

When the water reached the tepid limit of its potential, she hung her towel on the hook outside the stall and stepped in. The stalls, like much of Camp Horizons, were all in need of repair: mildew stained and grimy, the tile floors cracked and covered in green algae, which started growing in the damper corners and spread out like the tentacles of some monster. The flimsy stall walls were riddled with holes like a shoot-out had gone down. The conditions boggled her. Why were no repairs being done? Why had cabins been sealed off? Valid questions considering the amount of money being charged for the camp's services. A possible extra morsel of scandal for the article.

Lathering up, Erin relaxed and let the day

drift away while envisioning her soon-to-be finished article going viral. Garnering tweets of outrage that would lead to calls for action. And her name, her story, behind all of it. The crusted showerhead spurted erratically and pipes rattled from pressure. The stall's ongoing noise, along with her rampant thoughts, prevented Erin from noticing the Man moving past and ducking into the stall next to hers.

Erin's mind stayed on finding the opening line of the soon-to-be Pulitzer winning article; she worked on putting together a beast of a lead, some--thing catchy, powerful, that would grab the reader instantly. All she conjured were cheap-sounding clickbait titles, and they weren't what she wanted. Leaning against the side wall, Erin tried to enjoy the spray of warm water while the heat lasted, thinking only of her article, not realizing on the opposite side of her, the Man stood holding a pair of rusted, weathered garden shears.

At waist height, there was a hole which he slid the tips of the shears into before twisting them around, quietly carving a larger opening. Erin pushed herself away from the wall and absentmindedly moved around the stall. As she backed herself under the water to douse her hair, she continued fumbling over the words she chose. They jumbled around like loose puzzle pieces, and she wrangled them into a sentence only to discard all of it and try again. None of the lines sounded punchy enough to open what would be an explosive exposé.

As she backed up against the clean wall once again, she let the search for the opening line go and enjoyed the solitude. Not once noticing the now larger hole lining up directly with the base of her spine, nor the tips of the garden shears perched within, resting on the edge of the opening like a spider, patiently waiting for the moment to strike. Remaining against the wall, the shears twitched in their resting space, ready to lunge forward, but were forced to wait.

Erin needed her office, her creative space, and believed that was why she had trouble finding the right grouping of words. They would come tumbling out once she got back home with her favorite sandalwood incense going, cup of hot tea, and the filth of the horrible camp scrubbed off her permanently. Erin thought of her comfy office a hundred miles away and let out a deep sigh. No more wordplay for the night. The time had come to put Erin away and get Lisa ready again. As she prepared to step away and get back under the spray for a final rinse, the Man sent the shears forward with a forceful, penetrating thrust.

The intense pain shot up through Erin, taking her by surprise. For a moment, she remained frozen against the wall. Reaching a trembling hand behind her, she ran it down along her back, feeling her way until her fingers nicked the edge of the blade protruding from the wall. Whipping her hand back up, she found her fingers covered in blood. She unleashed a bone-chilling scream as the Man brought his hands together, snapping the garden shears closed. He fought briefly against the resistance Erin's spinal cord gave him, but once the blades joined together, the snap was satisfying. He yanked the shears back and ripped them out of Erin and through the wall.

Falling limply to the shower floor, Erin frantically slapped her legs and tried to get them to move. She punched at them wildly, not understanding why she couldn't feel anything when a moment ago there had been nothing but intense pain. Everything below her waist went lifeless. Weak screams barely rose above the creaky pipes and sputtering showerhead as the Man tore back the liner to the stall and stepped in. The bloody shears dangled at his side. Erin's screams lacked any ferocity as she dragged herself up against the rear wall. Her bottom lip trembled as she pleaded for him to stop. He raised the garden shears above his head. White, cloudy, and eerie, his eyes stared out at her from under the shadow the hoodie cast across his face.

Her hands went up in front of her in a reflex motion, one valiant final effort to save herself, but the blades pushed through them with ease. When the Man stepped back, Erin's body slumped against the shower wall, her hands crudely pinned to her forehead. Her fingers twitched, and her body shuddered as the life drained out of her.

Bob sat alone at one of the large picnic tables filling the mess hall. Like Karen, he preferred to eat after the evening's activities ended and when the Journeyers were close to lights out. She always kept a plate warm for him. Karen went about wiping down tables, despite most of them not needing any attention. No one had sat at them in months. Karen knew Bob long enough to understand after the night ended, he needed fifteen minutes of quiet decompression time to settle. But once the allotted time passed, she spoke. "Heard one of 'em went wild, had to go to the Hut."

"We've a spirited one on our hands, that's for sure." He put his spoon down, looking up at her round and kind face. "He reminded me of—*him*." Bob refused to say the name.

Karen stopped wiping the table and sat down across from Bob. He rarely mentioned the past, even though she'd been at Horizons with him in '95, '01, and again in '09, She volunteered to be the cook when Bob geared up to take over as director. Truthfully, his being camp director was only partly the reason she'd returned; the other was to get far away from the woman she worked with at the sporting good's store in North Lake Never. She'd confided to him that their attraction proved too strong, and Kelli began to reciprocate Karen's attention. "Are you're actually talking about, *him*?"

Bob's intense stare told her yes. "It's—what's that word always being thrown around—triggered, or is it triggering? I don't know, but it's bringing up stuff I haven't wanted to think about in a long time. From the moment that kid got out of the car he had this air about him that screamed—"

She stopped him before he uttered the name they swore never to mention. "That's ancient history, Bobby. He was a mess and sinner and brought all those issues on himself. And when the time came to pay, where was he? Up and ran off. He left, and we got better. End of story."

"You don't ever think about what happened to him?"

"No," she spoke curtly, sitting up and returning to her cleaning. "And you shouldn't either Bobby. Don't even say his darn name. Focus on the here and now and the young men and women we're helping come back to God."

Bob agreed with her but only since she didn't know the truth of that summer. She hadn't witnessed what he had all those years ago. "You're right." He dismissed the old topic and ushered in new business. "I have a question for you."

"Sure, Bobby, anything."

"Would you like to get married?" Bob studied her face, stuck midexpression between awkwardly smiling and questioning if his question were real, hoping he'd get a feel for her answer. "I know why we both came back here. I haven't fared well in any of my relationships lately, and I know you haven't either. It's hard out there for people like us."

"SSA's all the way!" Karen chanted as she threw her arms up like a cheerleader.

Bob chuckled, remembering the day they learned the term Same Sex Attraction being used at the camp, and when Karen first created the cheer during lunch. "When I'm here at Horizons, I know where I belong. I know what I'm doing. But out there, I'm a mess. I feel like I don't know anything. I get lonely. I get lost. And we know that leads to slipping, and gay is not the way."

He paused, his brow furrowing as he tried to remember the speech he'd prepared for this moment. "I think it'd be easier for both of us, wouldn't it? And it wouldn't hurt the camp's image if former Journeyers were now married and running Horizons as a happy couple." He rushed the last couple of words out before ducking his face back down into the bowl to slurp up a spoonful of Karen's ham-and-bean soup.

"We have a big problem." Kevin's deep voice cut through the silence before Karen gave any hint of an answer. Frantically, he rushed to where they sat, waving his phone.

"Kevin, we must lead by example. If we do not permit the—"

"We missed an important weather warning." Kevin flipped the phone around to show the weather app and the red circle hovering over the entirety of Lake Never. "A severe thunderstorm is about to drown us. And," he added reluctantly, "there is still no word on Killian and Matt. No sign of them anywhere. All their stuff is still in their lockers. What if they got hurt in the woods?" Kevin switched his gaze from Karen to Bob and back. "What if Killian wasn't seeing things?"

Five. That would make five Guides who had run off during Bob's short tenure. "There is no one out there," he declared as authoritatively as possible, sick of the murmurings about some mysterious stranger. "How long do we have until this storm hits us?"

"Killian said more than once someone was out there the past few nights walkin' around our camp. We still don't know who took those sweatshirts and hoodies from the storage closet. He went out there today specifically looking for—"

"Enough!" Bob's hands slammed down with enough force the spoon leapt from his bowl and landed on the table. "I've basically lived here a year and a half, and if there were someone around our camp, I would have seen them by now. The hoodies and sweatshirts are clothes. I'm sure they were taken by Jerome, Adam, or Aaron when they skipped out on us. Or maybe some random homeless person or a hiker, who wandered in and needed them. None of that makes me believe some nefarious person is out there lurking in our woods. Let us tackle the real issue—how long until the storm?"

"Within the next thirty minutes, and it's going to be bad for a couple hours. Should we call the police about Matt and Killian?"

Bob pushed his bowl away, no longer hungry. "They haven't been missing twenty-four hours, and Sheriff Doyle won't come out here until then. First thing in the morning we will call, and you, me, and Craig will go out and look for them. There is nothing we can do about them now, and we need to get prepared for a storm.

"Get the emergency gear pulled. Let's get the raincoats and flashlights prepped in the Guide's cabin, so everything is right there for us. There are extra batteries in the office if needed, and I will get the emergency candles from the storage closet. The Journeyers should be finishing evening prayer. Since they will be in lights out soon, they don't need anything. And we will still be doing checks," he added.

Kevin raised an eyebrow. "They're strongly advising us to stay inside, the visibility will—"

"We cannot leave Journeyers unattended all night, Kevin. Sin will get in." Bob's response was as serious as cancer. "In fact, it's been too long since they've been checked. Look in on them before start-

-ing storm prep. Everyone needs to be prepared to get a little wet tonight."

"What about Tyler?"

"Leave him," Bob said coldly. He rose from the table to both Karen and Kevin's questioning faces. *"Do not be deceived: God is not mocked, for whatever one sows, that will he also reap.* I'm sure by tomorrow he'll be far more willing to participate."

☠

The dense gray clouds gravid with rain rolled over the vast landscape encompassing Lake Never and unleashed their load upon the camp. The rain pounded on the tin roof of the Hut as Tyler sat zoned out, staring at the crude wooden door. He had no more energy to call for help. After hearing footsteps rustling around the Hut, he pounded on the walls and begged whoever might be there for help. After nothing happened, he turned his attention to the door and kicked at it. Defeated, he sat on the pillow as his head filled with every situation his mouthy attitude had ever gotten him into. The multiple offenses painted a clear picture of what being mouthier than needed and ruder than called for got him. While the situation sucked, Tyler didn't give a shit. Someone needed to say what the fuck needed to be said, and that was that. At the end of the day, he wasn't the one trying to brainwash people under the guise of Jesus.

The rain continued its onslaught. Deep, rolling thunder added some natural bass for the night's concert, masking the noise of someone approaching the Hut. Ty didn't register the knock on the door until a second bang came through louder than the first. Jumping to his feet, Ty's hands were up and ready to fight. For a brief moment in his head, an axe blade came bursting through the door, and behind the opening, a deranged Bob held the handle, spouting Bible verses and gearing up to hack the queerest parts right off him.

There was no axe. No Bob. But someone wrestled with the door as a nervous Tyler stepped closer. Hesitating for a moment, the fear winding up inside him, he put his ear against the wood and heard grunting. The door shook briefly before swinging open. Tyler braced himself for the worst, ready to swing if necessary. A wave of instant relief slapped against him when behind the door stood Chris. His soaked oversized shirt stuck to his chest, which rose and fell hypnotically from his labored breathing. His biceps bulged from the miniworkout it took to lift the two thick wooden bars placed across the doorway.

Tyler hugged Chris harder than he'd hugged anyone in a long time. The rain pelted them as Tyler thanked Chris over and over. Tears welled up in his eyes then rolled down his face, and he was happy they were camouflaged by the raindrops. Chris tightened his embrace and nuzzled against Tyler in return. "You came out here to save me?"

"Kind of—I need your help. Something isn't right with Jamal." The distress was telegraphed across slumped shoulders, a furrowed brow, and his bright, but heavy eyes. "They really locked you up in there." Chris showed him the door and how two wooden bars were secured and anchored with several bungee cords across the doorway.

"This place is fucked up," Tyler yelled, staring up at the sky as a massive clap of thunder rocked them.

☠

Myer sprung up from his bunk the moment Chris and Tyler entered the cabin. "You were supposed to be going to the bathroom. I'm reporting this." He angrily went to brush past them, his thin lips pursed and ready to send up the alarm. But Chris, a foot taller and forty pounds heavier, chest-bumped Myer into submission, forcing him to retreat to his bunk.

"Stay in there, and shut your mouth," Chris barked as he balled his fists and threatened Myer with them.

Tyler moved past the scene and found Jamal in one of the bunks toward the rear of the cabin; curled up, withdrawn, and solemn. Their eyes were red and bloodshot, and the stains of tears marked their face running from eyes to neck in splotchy rivers.

"They haven't spoken since we left First Night. It got rough after they removed you. I didn't know what to do, and you seem pretty smart. So, I thought maybe you'd know what would help." Chris guarded Myer, not allowing him to move from his bunk.

"What the fuck happened after I left?" Tyler crawled into the bunk and sat next to Jamal. They did not move, blink, nor acknowledge Ty's presence.

"Jamal," Ty said softly, making his voice as soothing and calm as possible. "It's okay." Jamal acknowledged him with a gentle glance in his direction before the vacant stare returned. "You're going to be all right. Do you want to talk about what happened? If you don't, it's okay. We're here for you whatever you need."

"My father..." Jamal whispered, their voice catching in their throat.

"What about him?"

"They told me I hated him, that I've hated him my whole life."

"Do you?" Tyler asked, not in a position to assume Jamal's feelings toward their parents were similar to his.

Jamal shook their head. "No," they muttered. "He sent me here and all, but he's being ignorant right now. He can't help it. Shit's been hard since Mom died, and I may not like him right now, but I've never hated him."

"They told us we all hate our fathers. And our mothers contributed to our queerness with their constant overbearingness," Chris added with a shrug. "Mine were normal until all this, so I don't know what he was talking about."

Tyler stretched his arm out toward Jamal, leaving his palm open, waiting in case they wanted to take it. "Jamal, they're trying to make you question who you are, so they can break you down and get you to accept that there is something wrong with you. It's the only way they can 'fix' us. This isn't who we are. This isn't who Jamal, whose last name I don't know yet is, because you are fabulous on levels I can't comprehend. There's no way anyone as magnificently wonderful as you are, is meant to be fixed. God doesn't make mistakes."

Jamal's brown-eyed gaze met his.

They raised up the right corner of their mouth slightly into the hint of a smile as their face softened.

"These aren't good people," Tyler continued. "They aren't following God; they follow words *men* wrote a long time ago. Some of those passages are great and bring healing and love to lots of people, but they're twisting this shit to justify hurting us."

"How did you know all those verses?" Myer inquired. "I'd assumed you'd never picked up a Bible in your life, let alone committed parts to memory."

"Know your enemy," Tyler retorted sharply, shooting Myer a dirty look. "You think I'm *not* going to read the book small-minded bigots keep using against me as their own holy weapon? No, I don't think so. I read the Bible—I committed parts to memory—so I could do exactly what I did tonight when some dick goes on a tirade of holiness. *My* God doesn't accept that shit."

"There is only one God," Myer nervously shouted before he flinched, clearly weary of Chris hitting him.

"Do you enjoy being wrong all the damn time? There are like 5,000 different religions on this planet. So, sorry—not sorry, I'm not listening to only one book on the subject. Jamal, *our* God loves you. They want to see you dance the fucking house down in your show. Right in the front row cheering you on, not judging. Not forcing you to change. Our God wants us to be happy, healthy, and most of all, kind. I think that's the secret to all of this; be a decent person and come from a place of kindness and love, but don't be afraid to beat an ignorant bitch's ass down if you need to." Tyler twisted his head in the direction of Myer, who retreated into his bunk.

"I don't know a lot," Tyler went on, "but I know holy people aren't supposed to lock teen boys in a hut and leave them in the middle of a raging thunderstorm. Holy people don't tell you you're a piece of sick garbage needing fixing. That's not godly. It's evil posing under the guise of something else. Jamal, remember who you were before you stepped into this fucking place."

The spirit moved within Jamal. The glimmer they held within their eyes sparkled once again. The muscles in Jamal's slender face loosened as their jaw unclenched and their shoulders dropped from their hunched position. Relief spread over them, and Jamal shook his arms of the last remnants of tension. Tyler's words had worked, and when Jamal grabbed his wrist and squeezed, Ty understood they weren't ready to speak, but they would be okay.

"Fuck!" Chris jumped back from the window and startled everyone. "Someone's coming." A yellow raincoat raced through the rain toward the cabin illuminated by a crack of lightning in the sky. "Tyler, hide." Chris pushed his fist under Myer's chin and promised his mouth would be wired shut for weeks if he uttered one word. "We were supposed to be praying." Chris went to get back to his bunk but didn't make it as Craig burst into the cabin, out of breath and drenched.

Tyler dove unnoticed into the bunk across from Jamal and hid under the blanket, keeping as low as he could.

"Chris, why are you wet?" Craig asked, sitting down at the table to regain his composure. "This is evening prayer hour, don't look like anyone is praying in here to me."

"I was taking a dump, and it started raining."

Craig ordered him to the back of the cabin to change while everyone else kept their eyes forward. Under his blanket, Tyler laughed; no matter how hard Craig tried, he failed to cover the natural effeminate qualities of his voice. When he walked them to First Night, Tyler observed how he constantly fixed his posture; from how he stood, to how he held his hands.

"We have a severe storm over us right now. Should be lasting a couple hours," Craig explained. Peeking slightly from beneath the blanket, Tyler observed the cabin as Jamal crawled silently out of one of the rear bunks and wiped their eyes, then moved to their own bed in the front. Craig pulled two candles out of his jacket. "It's eight thirty, so lights out. I'm leaving these here in case the power goes out and you need them. No more leaving the cabin for any reason," he ordered.

Chris walked back to the front in a dry shirt and crawled up into his bunk. "What about Tyler?"

"Tyler will be staying where he is for the night. Let his punishment be a lesson to the rest of you. If you do not choose to participate in your *Journey*, we will take corrective action. Tyler will rejoin us for morning prayer. Five thirty comes incredibly early, boys." Craig left the candles with nothing to light them with and exited the cabin. Chris crawled from his bunk the moment the door closed and went to the window, announcing after a tense moment that Craig was gone.

Tyler crawled out from under the blanket. "I have to go back," he said, feeling a slight flutter of butterflies in his stomach at the sight of Chris's warm, cute face. "But I'll need you to go with me. We have to put everything back."

Chris agreed, and without complaining, switched back into his damp shirt and shivered as the cold fabric pressed against his skin.

"Ya'll ain't seriously going back out there?" Jamal spoke up, seeming to finally feel well enough to.

"No choice. I want out of this place. But for now, we can't do anything except play along. Tomorrow we can find a way to get out here."

"Say what?"

"When I was out there in the Hut, I had a thought. The Guides have to have cars somewhere. They clearly don't live here year-round. They got to go to town at some point."

"And if we can steal one, we can get the hell out of here?" Chris moved toward the exit, liking what he heard.

"Go," Myer encouraged their plan from his bunk. "You are preventing me from getting better. I won't say anything about tonight or your plan. Go already, and once you're gone, it'll be God and me so I can get better and go back to my family."

"You can come with us if you want." Tyler's offer drew surprised looks from the others. "This is torture, Myer. This isn't therapy."

"No." Myer nestled into his bunk and turned his back toward them.

"Jamal, you okay?" Tyler wanted to be sure before he left.

"Yes, Boo, I'm good now. Thanks to you. I can't believe I let a couple of Bible-thumping

Saltines mess with my head like that."

Tyler blew Jamal a kiss and turned to Chris. "You ready? We'll have to be quick. I don't want you to get caught."

The handsome jock inched closer, letting his voice go soft as he shuffled his feet nervously on the floor. "I wouldn't mind being locked in the Hut with you." His face flushed as their gazes remained fixed, neither appearing to want to turn from the other until the invasive tap of Jamal's foot on the wood floor broke in.

"Girls, as cute as this is—we ain't got the time."

☠

The rain bombarded them in unrelenting sheets the moment Chris and Tyler exited the cabin. In an instant, their visibility went to zero, and they found themselves turned around. Chris, unsure which way would lead them back to the Hut, stopped under one of the three lampposts lining Harmony Lane. A bright jagged bolt of lightning illuminated the camp like the harsh pop of a camera's flash. Chris spotted the ladies' restroom. Sliding his hand in Tyler's, he pulled them in that direction. The Hut wasn't too much further, but they couldn't proceed until the storm eased up.

Chris swerved away from the direction he'd been following and pulled Ty into the restroom, both happy to be out of the mess as they shook the rain off. "We'll have to wait the storm out. I don't want us to get lost." Chris checked out the door, searching for any hint of the Guide's yellow rain slickers. "I don't know if I can find my way to the Hut in this. The location was hard to find the first time." He revealed he'd gotten lucky when he came across the Hut on his initial trip.

Tyler agreed. He didn't believe anyone would be out in the storm checking on them anyway. Running his hands through his hair, Ty scanned the restroom for a towel, spotting instead something odd sitting on the last sink in the row against the wall. Chris's head still craned out of the door, trying to see if anyone popped up within the flashes of lightning.

"Do you believe there's a car somewhere out there?" Chris asked, spinning around to see why there hadn't been as answer. Tyler appeared in front of him, cupping a hand over his mouth and pushing a finger to his own lips urging him to be quiet. Once Chris nodded he understood, Tyler moved his hand away and pointed to the last sink where a pink-and-yellow flowery toiletry bag sat on the sink.

"Oh shit, is someone in here?" Chris's voice shot up loudly, instantly forgetting why Tyler wanted him to stay quiet. "What do we—"

Ty narrowed his eyes, grabbed the jock's face, and pulled him into a kiss. The only remedy available to shut Chris up. Neither broke free from the embrace until Tyler, displaying an incredible amount of self-control, stepped back.

"Whoa," was all Chris uttered once separated. He stepped away, appearing dazed from the euphoria swishing through his body. Tyler expected someone to come rushing out from the showers, high on religion and waving a knife—but after a few tense minutes, no one did.

Ty had met one female, the cook, at dinner, and she didn't seem to be the type for flowery bags. Craig told him about the other female Guide, Lisa. Apparently, neither of them was there any longer, and the bag must have been left behind in the rush to get out before the rain started.

Keeping his eye on the doorway to the showers, Tyler found a spot on the floor, sat down, and rested his head against the wall. The day had been long and strange. "I think we're cool. If anyone were here, they'd have heard your loud ass." Tyler winked at Chris, who found a spot directly next to him.

Their knees touched, despite Chris's two-inch height difference, as they sat silently, trying to air dry while listening to the rain beat against the restroom's tin roof. The restroom became the only safe haven, and they found themselves anxious as they sat next to each other, both barely breathing, looking at each other before diverting their gaze away sheepishly as their bodies still hummed from the kiss.

Chris broke the silence first with a deep inhale before speaking. "Can I ask you something?"

"Sure, anything."

"When did you realize you were gay?"

Tyler gazed into the jock's deep-set blue eyes, which held beneath their luminous exterior a tidal pool of sadness and uncertainty. He wanted to kiss the pretty, unsure football player again and again until neither of them remembered where or who they were. "Fourth, maybe fifth, grade. All the boys were starting to pay attention to the girls. Trying to steal kisses after hitting them on the playground—I'll never understand straight dudes—but that shit wasn't for me. "I didn't know what being gay meant. I don't think I even knew the word for what I was; I knew I was different and that whatever made me different, I needed to keep to myself. I guessed when I didn't see anyone else acting like me—wanting to kiss a boy, wanting boys to like them—I figured something was wrong with me. What a bullshit world this is," he added, kicking at the air, mad at so many things he had no control over.

"You liked another guy back then?" Chris asked with a look of surprise. "I didn't even think about any of that stuff until the middle of high school."

Tyler felt bad he couldn't remember the name of the boy he'd spent the majority of class fawning over—a dreamy Italian boy who sat three desks away from him. From his olive skin to his jet-black hair and full pouty lips, he was all young Ty focused on. "I didn't know about sex, but I wanted him to kiss me. I wanted our lips to touch more than anything else. But I knew I couldn't go ask him, and so, I sat and stared and daydreamed. Flash-forward through a few awkward years, and I finally learned what being queer meant, and I had an epiphany. I was like, 'well that makes sense' and I went about the rest of my day.

"I have this issue; I had no problem being who I was. But this world seemed to have an issue with me, which pissed me off. People not liking me cause I jerk off to a different kind of porn is stupid. If you're going to hate someone, find a valid reason. Like those people who don't return carts, *they* deserve some fuckin' hate. But me? Hated for liking another guy when my life has nothing to do what them at all doesn't make any sense. It's why I'm angry all the time. All I've been doing is hiding and fighting against this world since realizing how this shit works."

Chris grabbed Tyler's hand and squeezed. "I'm so sorry you went through that. Sounds like it sucked."

Butterflies fluttered in Ty's stomach as he leaned forward, kissing him again. It was the first time anyone had showed him any sympathy for what he'd been through, and it sent the good kind of chills through his body. "It's okay. It's given me the very charming, friend-making personality I have today."

"I think you're charming, and I think you're angry about the right things. I should be angrier about the things in my life." Chris spoke through his dreamy daze as he comforted Ty before turning serious. "I've been distracted by sports most of my life. I'm good with a ball, and when my parents learned that, they pushed me to be the best, to get a scholarship, then go pro, and I loved all the attention. Sports kept me busy, so I didn't focus on anything except the team. I never found myself interested in any of the girls who liked me. I'd go out with them, of course. Ya know, cause it's what I'm supposed to do. My teammates were doing the same thing. I'd hang out, and sure, we'd do things, and I guess stuff felt okay. But I've never found one girl I truly enjoyed being with. I stayed focused on the team and didn't think much about anything else.

"And I'd never thought about Dion in that way until he started tutoring me." He paused on the name and grinned. "After our first lesson I couldn't stop picturing us together. And I don't mean just sex stuff but like chilling, or go to the movies, play some video games, take him to a ballgame, which would have been awesome. It didn't matter to me, I just wanted to be around him.

"I started getting nervous before he came over. Pacing my room like a crazy person while I waited, trying to figure out what I'd wear, how I'd look, which cologne to use. I guessed I was weird or something because no girl got me wound up in that way. I didn't know what to say, and I ended up staring at him the whole time. Not hearing anything he taught me because I was so lost in him. Imagining how he kissed, how his lips would feel against my skin. I know he caught me looking too, but I didn't know what he thought since I'd kind of bullied him when we were younger." His voice cracked at the remorse for his adolescent actions.

"And then he kissed me." The warmth of the memory softened Chris's face. "He'd asked me a question, and when I started thinking about the answer, he snuck in, and we kissed. It was amazing. And I kissed him back. The next time we, didn't pretend to study. We went right to jerking off together. That afternoon was like porn hot. Dion wouldn't let me touch him or anything. We only kissed. He said everything else we would have to work up to."

"What a tease. A boy after my own heart."

"I enjoyed our time together. And when he finally went down on me, I was blown away. I'd never enjoyed that before, you know. His mouth made me feel like I'd scored a winning touchdown at the Super Bowl. I was the MVP, a Heisman winner, first round draft pick, everything all rolled into one. And then my parents walked in and freaked the fuck out. Dion ran off. I got so confused, being with him didn't feel wrong, but they were acting like I'd murdered someone. I felt like such shit afterwards. In a weird way, I'm glad they sent me here."

"What the fuck for?"

"Because of you." Chris's face flushed and his heartbeat loudly enough, Ty could hear it. He adverted his eyes as he continued, "I've been picturing all those same things I did with Dion, and I know now what happened with him wasn't some fluke, cause I'm feeling the same about you. I'm gay," he spoke the words proudly. "I still don't know what that means exactly. And I don't know how I'm supposed to be now. I can't be like you, Tyler; you walk around so confident in who you are that I'm in awe, but I couldn't do that. I'm too scared things are going to change, and I won't be able to handle them."

Tyler ran the back of his hand across the baby-smooth skin of Chris's cheek and rubbed the pad of his thumb against the jock's pillowy lips. "Nothing's changed, cutie; you're still the same foosball-playing jock boy you've always been. The Chris you know isn't going away. None of what makes up who you are has changed, except you might be happier now."

"What about my friends, the other guys on my team?"

"Fuck 'em," Tyler proclaimed, waving those potential bigots away with his hands. "Your friends should like you for you. Who's blowing you shouldn't change their opinion, and if it does, fuck 'em. There are lots of people in this world. You'll make new friends. See, you've met Jamal and me already. And if you walk into the locker room and they act funny, it's because of their own insecurities. They probably think you're looking at them, judging them, or believing you want to fuck them in the same way they would if a girl walked in there.

"They're insecure, and don't bother trying to understand them either because straight people make little to no sense. You just be you, and when you play your foos-soccer-base-ball or whatever it is, they'll see how great you are." Tyler raised his arm as if he were toasting someone. "So, here's to you, Chris, whose last name I also don't know. Let me be the first to congratulate you for coming out. And I can't think of a better place to do so than at a gay conversion camp." Tyler covered a blushing Chris with another series of kisses.

Chris scooped Tyler up and pulled him over onto him. Ty wanted the parade of tender and equally passionate kisses to continue and move to the stripping off the jock's shirt and pants. A bolt of lightning lit up the restroom and within its flash, he once again saw the flowery bag sitting silently on the sink, and a wave of curiosity wafted over him demanding his attention drift away from Chris.

He patted his hands against his muscular chest, wishing they were somewhere with a bed and privacy. They weren't, however, and the urge to investigate forced him to stop. Much to a frustrated Chris's annoyance, Tyler broke their embrace and stood up cautiously. He walked down the row of sinks, and every few moments, the light show outside illuminated how grimy and in need of repair the restroom cabin was.

He found himself glad he'd not gotten naked and rolled around on its floors as tempting as the idea had been. After grabbing the bag, he checked inside expecting to see toiletries and nothing else. Instead, he pulled out a gray personal voice recorder.

"I witnessed them torture three young men today." Chris identified the female voice as Lisa, one the Guides Tyler hadn't met yet, and pointed out the jovial, Southern accent she'd spoken with on the first day was missing. "Maybe what they were doing wasn't torture in the traditional sense, but forcing three young men to spend seven hours praying in the hot sun without a break so they can, and I quote, *feel God's disappointment in them*, doesn't sit well with me. We're waiting on a last-minute arrival, and this activity is what Bob stated they will do until he arrives. He and the other Guides have repeatedly called them filthy, abominations, and mistakes. I've tried to find records of previous Journeyers, but so far, my unsupervised time in the office has been minimal. If they start this cycle, maybe I will be able to get in and get what I need. I'm sure someone is ready to talk on the record about the fuckery going on in this place."

Tyler's eyes sparkled with excitement at the blessing being dropped into their laps, and Chris's cute but vacant face revealed he'd not caught what the tape signified. Tyler wanted to kiss him again and again. "We need to find Lisa. She can help us."

☠

Craig stood in the doorway to the men's restroom cabin, watching the rain blot out his view, and decided he'd remain there. No point in running around in a storm to return to the Guide's cabin just to be ordered back out ten minutes later so Bob and Kevin could continue their game of gin rummy uninterrupted.

He didn't mind being stuck in the restroom. The rain on the tin roof had a calming effect on him, evoking memories of his childhood home in Tennessee. At thirty-four, those times were a whole other life. One where Craig found himself shamed in front of his family and kicked out at thirteen for not only being gay, but for a far worse offense—his effeminate nature. He did not know where, as his father put it, he'd picked up *that stuff.*

Craig hustled through life on the streets for a couple years, doing whatever it took to get by, until at sixteen, God led him to Horizons. He credited the camp with saving him from the unthinkable, and he begged then camp director, Chester Barrett, to help him find peace, promising he would find any way possible to repay him. Craig went through four cycles until deemed "straight", but the feeling of being cured remained elusive. No matter how hard he tried to lower his voice or subdue his delicate mannerisms, they always prevailed.

Seeing as he had the alone time, he reached into his back pocket and pulled out a rubber-banded group of dog-eared index cards. The top one read "affirmations" in Craig's neat handwriting. Moving to the row of sinks along the wall, he stared at himself in the mirror and prepared for the debasing exercise he'd repeated three times a day, every day, for the past ten years. Flipping the first card over he recited the contents while looking at and hating himself in the mirror.

"You are straight."

He shook his head, not enough confidence. Not enough masculinity. Repeating the card and lowering his voice another octave, Craig flipped through the affirmations, stating each one multiple times. "You are straight. You are strong. You are a forceful, virile male."

He struggled with the next card. "You love pussy." When the vulgar words did not flow out with the masculine inflection he'd intended, the frustration made his wrists go flighty, and he spun his hands like propellers. Craig set the cards down and backed away from the sink. Looking at himself, he saw only disgust and disappointment reflected back. He admonished himself loudly; he was nothing but filth. Inhaling deeply and with no hesitation, he brought his hand to his face.

"No." Craig shouted before he slapped himself, relenting only when his face and palm burned. His face now marked by handprints. Regaining his composure, he lifted the cards up and pressed on despite the stinging in his cheek.

"You *love* the vagina." Craig gave the words all the seriousness he could muster and did his best to make sure Daddy up in heaven believed him. "God loves you when you're a masculine man." Finally, his voice hit the low pitch desired, and his hands were still as statues.

His father's rough, smoker's voice still taunted him. "Look at Wishy-Washy Craig, the lil' queer with his limp wrists and that pinky sticking up

No son of mine is going to be a Wishy-Washy-Sissy Craig. No sir, no son of mine."

"Gay is not the way. Gay is not the way." Craig repeated Bob's mantra over and over, praying away whatever caused his accursed feminine affliction. "You are straight. You are masculine. You *loooove* the vagina." Craig underwent multiple techniques, which were supposed to have cured him, including a couple rounds of electric shock treatment, and nothing had done the trick. He continued his affirmations as he moved to the urinal. "Gay is not the way. Gay is not the way."

He was unaware of the Man hiding silently in the last stall, who upon hearing "gay is not the way," became enraged and emerged.

"You do not like men." Craig undid his pants and took himself in his hand as he willed away his queerness. "You *are* straight."

The Man stalked along the row of stalls with his right gloved hand grasped around an old electric drill. The tool had languished in the shed, but through the crusted crud covering the device, the green light signaling a full charge burned steadily.

Craig relaxed for a moment as he pissed. His free hand went limp, and he cursed his extremity, and himself, before delivering another series of harsh strikes to his face, making each one rougher than the last. "I am not a nasty queer."

The Man crept up behind Craig as the Guide continued his diatribe.

"Gay is not the way. Gay is not the way." Craig finished urinating and went to zip himself up. When he stopped, a shadow moved behind his own figure in the blurry reflection within the urinal's plumbing. Before he could twist around to check, the Man grabbed the back of Craig's head and in a violent, forceful thrust forward, Craig's mouth met the ceramic top of the urinal.

The Man then yanked him back and let Craig hit the floor spitting out mouthfuls of blood and broken bits of his own teeth. Scooting away, Craig stared at the assailant who towered above him. Revealing the drill in his hand, the Man pressed down on the trigger and jabbed the weapon in Craig's direction. At the end of the drill, the bit spun ferociously around, filling the room with the metallic grinding of the tool's motor.

Craig tried to yell, but the pain paralyzed his voice, and he knew no one would be able to hear his garbled cries over the storm. For every three feet Craig tried to slide away, the Man took a single step forward, reeving the drill. The noise taunted Craig, and with every whir of the motor, and the sight of the massive drill bit spinning, his body tensed. "Please," he begged, "I've not done anything to you. I don't even know who you are."

Craig twirled his hands, waving defeat and hoping for mercy. But his limp jazz-hands did nothing to sway the Man who pressed the trigger again and brought the drill down. The flat two-inch bit dug into Craig's leg, pulverizing the muscles in his calf as it bore a hole into them. The Man held the drill in place for a solid thirty seconds, allowing the bit to do its business, before pushing in deeper.

In an instant, Craig's pant leg soaked through with blood. A second wave of intense pain flooded his poor body, and he had no time to acknowledge it before his attacker struck again.

The Man retracted the drill, letting its bloody bit spin, spraying the room with red mist.

The face of his attacker was hidden from Craig's view; the top half from the nose up was concealed by the shadow of the hoodie. He recognized the arms of a yellow Camp Horizons sweatshirt, two of which were torn off and now covered the bottom half of his face like a scarf.

His eyes drifted from the hooded face to the Man's body where he noticed the sweatshirts and hoodies he wore also belonged to the camp. They were the same ones believed to have been stolen and were shredded and torn, layered over one another, and on top of them were three hoodies. All with their Camp Horizons logos ripped and covered with dried mud.

Craig weakly held his hands up in front of him, begging for his life. "I didn't do anything to you. Why are you doing this?" the Guide cried, unaware of what crime he'd committed. The Man corrected his posture as he stood over Craig, the drill by his side with its bit still spinning anxiously for more flesh, his finger pumping the trigger. There was a moment, albeit brief, in which Craig believed the Man would stop. As Craig went to prematurely thank God—the Man flung forward.

The drill bit grabbed the skin of Craig's palm and spun, ripping the flesh from the hand before tearing through the meaty palm with reckless abandon. The bit snagged the thick median nerve, which snakes its way through the entire hand and up the forearm, and with a violent motion yanked the nerve directly from the body. The tendril whisked around on the bit before flying off and sticking to the wall behind Craig.

The drill bore through the backside of Craig's hand and sprayed his face with hot blood. In his final minutes, all he could recall was the last time he'd been on a floor and hot bodily fluids had been flung in his face. He enjoyed that night more than he ever allowed himself to admit. Bemused and helpless, he gazed through the ragged opening in his hand as his killer approached him. But there was no strength left to fight back. The drill bit swooped in like a bird of prey and pulverized his left eye, blending the contents of the socket around like a mixing bowl until viscous pink fluid leaked out down his face.

Craig ceased screaming. As had been true throughout his whole life—no one was listening anyway. For once, he stopped feeling; the more he let go, the less the pain overtook him. With no reason to hold on anymore as the Man continued to puncture his body with holes, Craig let the world around him go dark. The final rattling in his ears, sounding like a clunky can falling down a flight of stairs, was the drill's whirring old motor as the bit obliterated his right eye.

☠

Tyler tried his best to restrain himself, but Chris's lips were irresistible, and the past thirty minutes they'd spent kissing proved his skills extended beyond throwing a football. Tyler prepared to take a deep breath and dive in for more when the rain pounding the roof began to let up, the substantial part of the storm passing.

"Okay, okay." The words were more a directive to himself as he patted Chris's chest, wishing he could rip the shirt off, and pushed the jock away. "They might check on us now that it's let up." The thought of leaving Chris and returning to the Hut pissed him off, but if they were going to find Lisa and persuade her to help them, everyone needed to be in their places.

As they stood and straightened themselves out, they heard another source of running water, one covered by the storm and not the rain against the roof but—the showers. Ty's eyes flashed with curiosity. No one would have showered throughout such an intense storm. Dragging a reluctant Chris along with him, Tyler realized they'd not checked the whole bathroom. They'd gone by an assumption the place was empty. He wasn't concerned; if it were Lisa, they could talk to her now instead of struggling to find a private moment later.

And while Chris stood taller, bulkier, and stronger, he clung to Tyler's thin swimmer's frame, his head nestled closely against Ty's shoulder. As they neared the corner, they peered down the row of shower stalls to the one with a light on and its curtain pulled back.

"Think she's been here this whole time?" Chris whispered into Tyler's ear before taking the opportunity to give him a playful kiss.

"Maybe she thought we were one of them." However, nothing explained why she left her toiletry bag, and more so the incriminating recorder, out and unattended. "Um...hello, Lisa?"

When he investigated the next-to-last stall, his voice, amped to release a terrifying cry, did an about-face in his throat. Tyler's mouth stayed agape as his eyes fell upon the handles of the garden shears with their deteriorating black rubber grips, breaking away tiny piece by tiny piece. The shears' rusty blades were no longer visible, having been forced as far as possible into Lisa's skull.

Tyler spun around into Chris's arms and tried to look at the ground, but the bloody mess from the shower seeped out over their sneakers. Chris pulled them away from Lisa's body, through the restroom, and out into the rain.

☠

After Kevin's frantic entrance and Bob's quick exit, Karen found herself alone in the kitchen, cleaning up when the bottom fell out over the camp. She did not mind the solitude since it gave her time to ponder Bob's proposal.

Washing the last of the lingering dishes, her mind drifted over the pros of being married to Bob: No more hounding from her family on why there wasn't a man in her life, the sole topic of discussion whenever she visited. Marriage would get her parents off her back and create a reliable home life with someone who understood her background and the unique challenges of living in the world as an ex-gay. Bob would help her stay on God's path, and she'd help him do the same. Maybe with Bob, there would finally be the loving home she'd always dreamed of having.

As she dried the dishes, she thought about the cons: What would Bob expect from her as a wife? Cooking? Cleaning? All those archaic roles of a wife the church loved reaffirming. Karen cursed her homosexuality, and as much as she loved God, she'd no intention whatsoever of being nothing more in this world than someone's *wifey*. And the biggest con: What he would expect in the way of marital relations?

Karen slept with men, but the coupling usually occurred right after finishing her Journey at Horizons. She'd find the first interested man and bed him, proving to herself and God she was cured. Those relationships failed to last past a month, and Karen never found herself comfortable enough to tell any of those men the truth about herself or Horizons. But a man had been on her and in her, which should have been enough for God, she hoped. Boyfriends were good at keeping her family's questions at bay, but they were fewer and far between as she got older.

Pacing the mess hall, listening to the rain and thunder put their show on, she thought about sex— more specifically, sex with Bob. What bothered her was Bobby had been her friend since their teens and he knew all her secrets and fears and she his. But nothing romantic had ever bloomed between them. If he did not want sex, then marriage might be genuinely appealing, and there'd be no reason to decline his offer. From where she sat at one of the tables, the kitchen was visible, and the pantry's slatted door grinned like a lover beckoning her. She'd hoped to reach a decision *without* having to resort to the pantry's help. Trapped by the storm and with debates running in her mind, the snacks proved too tempting to resist. Karen pulled up the chain she wore around her neck as she entered the kitchen and thumbed the single key in her right hand. The pantry itself didn't need a key, nothing to protect in there, past the standard canned goods, soup packets, and off-brand snacks for the Journeyers. Hidden under the bottom shelf and pushed back enough to not be in eyesight, she retrieved a small, padlocked footlocker.

Using the key, she flipped the top open, revealing her personal treasure trove of sweet and salty name-brand snacks and name-brand food she kept for the Guides. The prized possession: the real Kraft Mac and Cheese she made for them once a week while the campers enjoyed the generic off-brand variety none the wiser. She snatched up three mini bags of Fritos and two handfuls of small Dove chocolates before locking up the treasure chest and pushing the footlocker back under the shelf.

Sitting at the kitchen's island, Karen dug into the bags of chips and wondered about Bob, marriage, and sex. Why had he asked her out of the blue? They had known each other since they were teens, but she'd only ever been to his apartment four times for a social gathering. Would he want to live there? Would they be married but live separately? Look for a new home? He hadn't been exaggerating when he told Kevin he basically lived at Horizons; it was the truth, and while she loved the camp, she'd no plans to live on the south side of Lake Never all year.

Needing a drink to wash down the salty chips, Karen opened the fridge and found herself staring at the sodas, uncertain of which one to choose. The choice wasn't as simple as quenching her thirst. Now she had to know if a full-on wedding would be going on. Would she be getting into a dress? Would there be photographers and a huge party with all eyes on her? If so, the dieting needed to begin. As much as she hated giving up carbs, a diet soda would be the symbolic first step. But if the wedding were nothing more than a quickie ceremony at the courthouse, then no need to stress, and she would enjoy the full-sugar variety.

Her thoughts having trailed off from the decision at hand, Karen didn't realize she'd held the fridge door open an alarmingly long time. Long enough that if a killer happened to walk in, as one had, she'd have made it easy for them to creep up and stand menacingly behind it, ready to strike the moment she closed the door. The debate raged over diet or regular soda in her mind, and she gripped the fridge handle and absentmindedly swung the door softly back and forth until she gave in and grabbed the red can. She closed the door without incident and returned to the island. Either way, a decision did not have to be made tonight, and the diet could start another day, maybe. She guzzled down the drink, loving the sting of the ice-cold carbonation tickling her throat.

There may not have been a killer behind the fridge door ready to pounce on her, but the Man was hiding in the mess hall. His entrance had been concealed by thunder and his own unearthly aura of silence. Standing in the far corner, he stalked Karen the whole time she pondered her life choices. As she moved about the well-lit kitchen, then settled in at the island and devoured her snacks, he began to slink along the wall and arrived at the doorway to the kitchen, still unseen.

The snacks were gone, and no real comfort or conclusion had come from their aid. Karen collected her wrappers and threw everything away, making sure to put the candy and chip bags under the other nondescript trash. No one needed to know about the secret stash; if they did, the Guides would be hounding her after every meal. The day had proven to be a long and tiring one, aches of exhaustion finally showing themselves in her shoulders along with the growing hum of a headache at the base of her neck from unanswered questions, uncertain futures, and an implosion of too much sugar.

Looking out into the mess hall, Karen expected to see, as she had a hundred times before, the collection of picnic and circular tables, the small stage where they conducted the food blessings for every meal, and the American flag hanging proudly on the pole in the far corner despite being faded by the sun.

Instead, nothing but darkness filled the doorway. From within it, the Man stepped forward with a hook in his hand. Startled, Karen backed against the sink and reached behind her to grab the large butcher knife from the rack of drying dishes.

"I don't know who you are, buddy. But boy, did you pick the wrong darn cabin."

Not waiting for the figure to make a move, Karen rushed forward with the knife held up, ready to stab him quick and get out of there. As she came at him, he swatted her away with a casual swish of his arm and knocked the knife to the floor. On his return swing, he sent his hand across Karen's face with a solid smack that rocked her on her feet. Wasting no time, she threw her leg up and her foot landed square between his legs with a deafening thud. As she stepped away, satisfied with her action, she waited for him to fall over, moaning in pain. But the Man remained still, upright, and unresponsive. Before Karen questioned what happened, the hook swung at her again. She ducked out of the way, jumped onto the island and tried to scoot herself across to the other side. She wasn't fast enough. The tip of the hook caught her deep in the calf. As soon as the hook and her skin connected, the Man ripped the weapon down the length of the muscle. Karen screamed, feeling the bisected skin flapping against her leg as she wiggled away, tumbling to the floor.

The obligatory screaming in horror came next as she scrambled toward the door, the mandatory pleading for her life as she cowered. The Man cared not for anything she said as he grabbed her neck like a chicken ready for slaughter. Karen stopped trying to fight him off when he lifted her hefty frame off the floor and held her the full length of his reach as if she weighed nothing. He whipped her through the air and slammed her down on the island with such force, the blow bent each of island's metal legs inward and the table buckled in the center.

The light fixture swung above Karen as she tried but failed to focus on the glowing bulb. His presence loomed over her, she wet her lips about to speak but was not given the opportunity. The hook cut through the air hot and violent. When the sharp tip came down it snagged her at the bully button. He dug in before yanking the hook the length of her torso, ripping through her body as easily as someone zipping up their jacket, until the hook exploded out of her throat in a glorious and bloody show.

☠

Okay.

    Okay.

Tyler repeatedly told himself he was fine over his own labored breathing. His eyes fell on everything around him: the still-pouring rain, his white sneakers getting muddier as they trudged toward the cabin, and Chris's hand in his pulling him forward. While he recognized these sights, none of them registered. Superimposed over everything was the image of Lisa's dead body with her hands brutally pinned to her own head by the garden shears.

    Lisa had not merely been killed—she'd been punished. Tyler broke from Chris's grip, no longer able to move forward, not caring the rain pelted him. He repeated to himself that things were okay over and over in his head, coaching himself, trying to recall the calming breathing techniques he'd learned from YouTube. Hiding his queerness from Michael and Nadine resulted in lots of anxiety and the occasional panic attack, and since coming out to them had been out of the question, he'd found ways to cope. Yet no one sent them to a camp to be better parents.

    But that didn't matter. What mattered was who killed Lisa. Someone in the camp? Had a local homophobe gotten fucked up and decided to go out and have some fun? Or—despite his attempts to shake the disturbing thought off, it anchored in his head—the killer was one of the Guides. Had they learned she was a journalist investigating their camp? Did one of them kill her because of it? The idea they would commit murder sent chills down Ty's already cold, wet spine. If one of them did that to her, what would they do to them?

Looking around at his surroundings, Tyler swore he spotted *them* behind every tree; one of them with their face hidden behind a mask of human skin, brandishing a chainsaw in his hands. A tall figure in a hockey mask with an axe. A human shape with a pale-white blank face, and a large knife. And all wearing bright-yellow Camp Horizons shirts, watching, waiting for their moment to pounce. They were not real, but the threat they represented was, and Ty feared what would happen if they found out he and Chris discovered Lisa's body.

Reaching out, he again found and held Chris's hand, knowing for sure he was real. They had to move. Tyler pulled Chris in and kissed him, not knowing what would happen next but needing one more hit of the good stuff before they faced the rest of their night.

Myer filled the cabin with his prayers, making sure Jamal heard him boisterously ask God for forgiveness not only for himself but for the heathens he shared a room with. Once he tired himself out and went to sleep, Jamal removed the earplugs and muffled a laugh at the fact Myer's preaching truly fell onto deaf ears. Not one word of his mini sermon had gotten through.

As quietly as possible, Jamal grabbed the pillows from one of the unused bunks and fashioned a makeshift body as a stand in for Chris. Jamal hoped the dummy would be enough to fool anyone who checked on them but wasn't sure the rouse would hold up against closer inspection. They took to pacing the aisle, worried Chris hadn't returned. With every passing moment, Jamal became convinced something had gone wrong. Perhaps they'd been caught? Jamal's foot never stopped shaking as they sat cross-legged at the table by the door, waiting anxiously like a parent.

"You shouldn't sit like a woman." Myer groggily walked past, startling Jamal, who did not realize the annoying one had risen. "You're a man, aren't you?"

"Bitch, take your scrawny ass back to bed. I am *me*. Why you mad about it? And I'll be whoever the hell I want to be when I wake up in the morning, Myer, and no one is going to force me into some category cause that makes things easier for 'em. Not today. Not tomorrow. Not ever."

Myer groaned, "whatever. Save your gender equality speech for people who care. I've never heard of a girl named *Jamal*." He spoke flat and monotone to make their name as unattractive as possible, and was proud of himself as he did.

Jamal's eyes fired with anger as they pointed their finger at Myer. "Boy, you best get my name out of yo' mouth. That's one. And two, don't you ever disrespect the name my mother gave me. She passed before I came into my truth, and since she isn't here to discuss a new name with me, I will keep the one she gave me. Jamal suits me fine." That time, the name came armed with appropriate flair and panache it deserved. Jamal stood up, finally noticing

Myer hadn't gotten up to chat. "Where the fuck you think you goin', Saltine?"

"Calm down Laquifa. I need to use the restroom." Myer sneered at Jamal as he grabbed the flashlight off the table before checking outside. The rain still poured, but nowhere near as bad, and he'd ignored the call of nature long enough. "And don't worry, I'm not telling on you sinners...*tonight.*"

Jamal fumed as Myer ran off toward the restroom. Once Chris got back, he would deal with Myer, and Jamal would happily watch the scrawny oh-so-holy boy get pounded on and not in the fun, sexy kind of way either. They returned to the chair and got settled in, expecting to be waiting for longer, when the door swung open and slammed against the side of the cabin loudly. Jamal shot out of the chair, ready to swing, only to find Chris and Tyler, who rushed in from the rain.

"Girls, bustin' in here like the po-po is a no-no, okay? The fuck wrong with y'all?"

"We found one of the Guides dead." Tyler spoke through his breathlessness, checking around the room for anything to block the cabin door with since there was no working lock.

"What?" Jamal expected to hear any number of things as an explanation to what happened, but a dead Guide wasn't on the list.

"She's like dead-dead." Chris skipped the gruesome details as he explained what they'd found in the restroom.

"And y'all sure this wasn't some kind of an accident?"

"No," Tyler shouted, "definitely not a fucking accident."

Jamal, still fired up from their interaction with Myer, wasted no time flipping the wooden chair over and putting a foot through the spokes along the bottom. They snapped off one of the broken legs and discarded the chair on the floor. "I ain't dying in these fucking woods," Jamal announced, gripping their homemade club.

Tyler admired their spirit, and if they got through the night, they would be forever friends. "Let's get this place barricaded."

Before they found the first item to push in front of the door, Myer's screaming forced a stop. A moment later, disheveled and frantic, he dashed out of the rain and bolted up the stairs and into the cabin, terrified and sounding like a banshee. "Dead...in the restroom." He barely got the words out through his dramatic wailing.

"Girl, we already know she dead, why you yellin'?" Jamal gripped their weapon, hoping Myer gave them an excuse to use it.

"Her? What?" Myer asked confused as he shook his head. "No, Craig."

☠

They moved from their cabin in a tight formation, shoulder to shoulder, with eyes out on the woods surrounding them. They made their way to the restroom where the light from the flashlight shook in Tyler's trembling hand as it landed on Craig's mangled body. His head was slumped over, and the hollow sockets where his eyes once were stared back at them. His body littered with dozens upon dozens of still bleeding puncture wounds.

"Oh, fuck that, this is some White people nonsense right here." Jamal grabbed at their stomach and spun away from the gory scene.

"And how exactly did you deduce the murderer's race, Mrs. Fletcher?" Myer asked, stopping everyone for a moment with his single and only quip of the evening.

"Listen, boo-boo, I'm from the ATL, and I've seen some shit. But this here, this is that next-level horror movie style fuckery, and that usually means serial killer—or killers plural—and those, my Pumpkin Spiced Cinnamon Saltine, are predominantly what? Yes, ma'am. Caucasian males. And with that, this fabulous unicorn of color is getting the hell up out of Horizons." Jamal made their way to the door, shaking their head and waving their arms with a flourish while complaining about the white nonsense surrounding them.

"What is going on?" Chris remained by the doorway; one gruesome murder was enough for his stomach for one night.

Tyler wished he knew, but the thoughts bombarding him were not good ones. Craig seemingly met the same fate as Lisa—his body brutalized beyond belief. Tyler spent enough Sundays binging true crime docos and podcasts to know that meant they were dealing with a heated, angry killer who was probably out of control.

"I know none of us did this." He addressed the other three, feeling somehow, he'd become the leader of their tiny enclave. "And that means we can only trust the people standing in this room." Four sets of eyes darted back and forth between them all.

Tyler worried his thought about the killer

being one of the Guides may have been wrong. If it were Lisa's body alone, maybe, but what had Craig done? In the small amount of time Tyler had spent with him, he knew the Guide committed himself to drinking the Horizon's Kool-Aid. Their killer was someone else.

"I feel someone is watchin' us for real, boo-boos. Do you think some crazy fool wandered in from the woods?" Jamal asked, staring out into the rain. Tyler didn't want to respond to the question because frankly, the answer scared the shit out of him. But Jamal repeated their concern twice, giving him no option.

"Yes," he fretted. The fear he'd applied to the Guides coming for them transferred. "If it's someone from outside, I think they're taking out the Guides first, and maybe coming for us next." Tyler glanced at Chris, the last thing he wanted would be something happening to his new flame. Or his fabulous new friend. And while his experience with Myer was rocky, he didn't want anything to happen to him either.

"What if it's Bob or Kevin?" Chris asked.

"I don't know, maybe," Tyler confessed, truly at a loss and ignoring the scowl from Myer, who he knew refused to believe such accusations.

"Can't we just go?" Jamal asked as if the option hadn't occurred to anyone else. "Like walk the fuck up out of here?"

"We're being punished," Myer spoke softly at first, but when no one acknowledged him, he began talking louder. "God is punishing us. I can't stay here with you heathens. None of you took this seriously, and you wouldn't listen to God's word, and now look at this—he is punishing us." Myer moved closer to the door.

Tyler tried to keep his voice as friendly as he could, knowing now was not the time for them to divert into an argument. "No, God didn't do this, some sick fucker did."

Myer refused to accept Ty's explanation with a shake of his head. "God spoke to me yesterday. He told me this is where I belong, but not with you. Not with your lies, your fake sincerity. I need to go." He moved past Chris, unafraid as he stood in the doorway.

"Myer, it's not safe out there. We'll be okay if we stick together," Tyler promised, believing the lie himself. If they stayed together, they would make their escape from Horizons.

"It's not safe with *you*," Myer yelled. "You never took this seriously. You've mocked God from the moment you showed up with your cocky attitude like you're so right, and we're all wrong. But you're nothing but a filthy sinner. And what's worse is you love it." Myer threw his arms down. "I need to get away from you people."

"*You people*?" Jamal said aghast, grasping at their imaginary pearls.

As Myer went to leave, Tyler tugged his sleeve softly, urging him to remain with them.

"Get your filthy hands off me, you sick faggot." Myer pulled himself away from Tyler's grip, visibly disgusted he'd been touched. A nanosecond later, Ty's fist slammed against the side of Myer's face, sending him to the ground. Instant regret flooded Tyler, but that F-word was triggering, and he leaned down hastily to apologize for his actions.

"Myer, I'm sorry. Please...don't go out there."

With a look of pure untapped hatred burning from him, Myer rubbed his jaw and got to his feet before running out into the rain.

Tyler chased after him, shouting more apologies, feeling worse with every step for the punch he'd thrown. "Myer, please stay with us." He kept his distance when Myer skidded to a stop on Harmony Lane and looked around wildly, clearly unsure of which way to go.

"You don't understand." Myer's pent-up frustration carried over the rain as it poured out of him. "I want to go home. I want to see my family. I need them to love me again, and they won't, not until I'm better. Don't you get I don't want to be gay?"

"Myer, dammit, they should love you anyway. They should love *you* for you." Tyler's mind worked hard to find the right combo of words that would help persuade Myer to stay. But his words failed him when he spotted a tall, hooded figure stepping out from behind the trees—seemingly out of thin air—and walking toward them.

"This is a sickness!" Myer ranted unaware of the danger approaching him. "A sickness I'm tired of. Aren't you? Aren't you tired yet? Why do we keep making our lives harder than they have to be just because we're different? I don't want to live some nasty queer lifestyle anymore. I need God to love me. I need my family to love me."

Fear's icy fingers squeezed Tyler's gut tightly. He shouted and waved frantically, desperate to get Myer's attention, but the boy appeared lost within his own *Lifetime* movie moment. The Man stopped behind the ranting Myer, reached into the many layers covering his frame, and removed a large, serrated hunting knife. He raised the knife in the air above Myer.

With his eyes closed, Myer turned his face up toward the sky. "God will love me again. God will bless me by taking my affliction away. And when I'm in my Lord's good favor again, I will be healed. I will come back to help others find their way from this disgusting life. See me, my savior," he went full-fanatic as he pleaded to the heavens. "See me and heal me."

The rain splashed against Myer's face like a vertical baptism, washing away his sins. And as he opened his eyes, the stranger's arm was raised above him—the knife poised to strike.

"Please..." Myer whimpered, his gaze locked onto the gleam at the end of the blade, his lips trembling as he spoke again.

Tyler couldn't make out Myer's final words over the noise; they were either "don't" or a weakly mumbled "do it." Ty wasn't sure, and regardless of which, the knife came down. The blade disappeared into Myer's shoulder, who screamed but his vocalizations were quickly cut short. The Man's hands grabbed both sides of Myer's head at his ears and jostled him around as the pressure on his skull increased. Myer's body convulsed, his eyes rolling up into his head as the whites of them flashed out at Tyler as his mouth fell open. With one forceful push, the contents of Myer's head exploded out of the top as if his skull were a pus-filled boil being popped. The Man removed the knife and tossed Myer's body to the ground before facing

Tyler.

"Please dude." Tyler threw his hands up, showing he meant no harm. "I don't want to die in this shithole."

The Man's menacing stance softened. His shoulders dropped, and he tucked the knife away in his layers of clothes. An odd acknowledgment to Tyler's request, which he didn't believe happened until the Man's attention returned to Myer's body and he dragged the dead boy off into the woods.

"What the fuck?" Tyler exclaimed, confused at the turn of events. As the fear paralyzing him subsided, two strong arms grabbed him from behind and pulled him into the restroom.

☠

Bob stomped away from the empty Hut, angrier than a kaiju rampaging Tokyo. Strict instructions were left that no one was to check on Tyler until sunrise. Bob wanted him to feel the lonely emptiness a homosexual life would eventually bring him. The longer in the Hut on the first offense, the more eager a Journeyer would be to get on the straight and narrow.

In two hours, the storm successfully scattered his entire staff, and he did not know where anyone was. He'd been playing gin rummy in the Guide's cabin with Kevin during the duration, and everyone had split up. Bob knew the rebellious boy hadn't run off. No, he was too smart for that. He'd probably used the storm to sneak off for some fun with one of the other Journeyers. Bob spotted the way Chris eyed Tyler during his First Night tirade with the dopiest lovelorn eyes he'd ever seen. He knew Chris had been ready to spring out of his chair when Kevin and Craig grabbed Tyler and dragged him away.

Not wanting anyone to see him catch Tyler by surprise, Bob followed an older, unmaintained dirt trail only those familiar with the camp from the '90s knew how to navigate. The trail ran along the side of the camp and was hidden from the more established paths. Bob planned to sneak around the long way and come up behind the boys' cabin. Catching Tyler in any sexual act would allow for stricter punishments.

The unnamed path ended at Salvation Trail, which snaked down along the side of camp until dead-ending into Heavenly Path where Bob stopped. Down Heavenly Path to the left led further into the forest and ended at a large sycamore tree. Bob had not ventured out there since returning as director. Down that path were memories of a horrible night from long ago, memories he did not want to recall and fought hard to bury.

To the right, the path curved along the shore of Lake Never before looping around and heading toward camp. Bob would follow the trail past the two vacant cabins and cut along Harmony Lane onto another older, unmaintained path, which would go past the defunct archery range, around more vacant boarded-up cabins, and up behind the boys' cabin. A hike indeed, but one he would not regret as every step filled him with certainty Tyler had coerced Chris into some sexual shenanigans.

One of the Journeyers let Tyler out. Not Myer, of course. No, Myer arrived there with the same spirit Bob had. He understood Myer's frustration with his fellow Journeyers. He'd dealt with the same during his time—until that night.

Refusing to indulge the ghosts of the past, who seemed anxious that night to make themselves known, he focused on the rain's intensity, which finally eased into a light sprinkle. Bob hiked up past the first vacant cabin and shone the flashlight at it as he passed. He checked to see that the door remained boarded up and none of the windows were broken. The drop in Horizons' attendance forced four out of the seven sleeper cabins to be closed, and heartbroken Bob found himself forced to juggle the cost of maintaining each cabin and running the camp with money they simply didn't have.

The circular beam of light danced along the wet ground before shining on the next cabin. Bob stopped and kept the light on the door. The board across the doorway to keep it shut had been pried off and hung loosely from a single nail, mocking the poor carpentry skills of whomever had secured them.

Gotcha. Bob made himself as quiet as possible as he snuck inside the cabin. The rain had soaked the floor by the door, and Bob tried to move through the puddle without making a sound. He covered the flashlight's beam with his hand and waited for the right moment to unleash the holy light on whoever hid in there as he crept down the center aisle toward the back.

Lightning flashed, and Bob made out figures gathered closely to one another in the last set of bunks. A smell tickled his nose, something foul. Brushing the scent off as mildew or mold within the damp cabin, he proceeded inward, readying himself to pounce and catch the vile offenders. Bob's face beamed with unearned righteousness—the kind people of Bob's ilk tended to have as if he alone were charged by God to personally shine the holy light upon the sinning youth, catching them amid their sinful delights.

"God sees you," he shouted triumphantly, leaping from the shadows as he removed his hand and flooded the rear bunks with light. The bright circular orb fell on the figures sitting there, and instantly, he learned these were not the fornicating youths he'd been so confident they were. Instead, Bob had found his own collection of missing Guides.

In the left bunk, Matt and Killian's bodies were positioned in a lover's embrace. Matt snuggled up against Killian, his head resting on the taller Guide's shoulder. Bob's eyes avoided the gaping wound, fracturing Matt's face down the center. He found more horror at the sight of Killian's dismembered head crudely affixed onto the end of a snapped-off broom handle forced down the opening in his neck. Killian's purple and bloated face had been manipulated postmortem to give him an O-face as best managed; his eyes were rolled up into his head, his mouth rigged open with a small stick to mimic a moan. In his exposed lap, Matt's fingers gripped the dead Guide's ample manhood, and he'd been propped up to look as if he were in the midst of a hand job. In his own lap, his hand laid where a penis should be, except there was none. Matt's crotch had been mutilated, his phallus and testicles sawed off and placed in his outstretched hand as if offering them up to Bob.

Disgusted, Bob fought down the vomit racing to be wretched up as he stepped away from the bed. "My God in heaven." He spun away from the perverse atrocity only to face the bunk behind him, and when the flashlight hit the beds, Bob's mouth opened—vomit, not screams, raced forward.

Jerome, the first Guide Bob hired, a devout young man ready to serve, eager to help others, was naked and rotting with a pickaxe lodged deep into his skull. Positioned across his lap was Adam, with his stomach cavity splayed open to the world, and Jerome's penis stuffed into his decomposing mouth. Behind him and made to look as if he were taking Adam from behind, was—Bob assumed—the youngest of the missing Guides, Aaron. But the face's mangled flesh, pulverized muscles, speckled with white flecks of bone fragments, created a gore-soaked meatloaf, no longer holding any identifying features. If not for the yellow shirt he wore, Bob wouldn't have known.

Bob fumbled away from his Guides in their unholy positions and cried out for help from his creator, unaware the Man stood at the far end of the cabin gripping a bloodied axe, enjoying Bob viewing his artistic handiwork.

Bob lowered his head and started for the exit but stopped when he saw a figure at the far end of the cabin. He flashed the light into the stranger's face, and two eyes eerily shined reflectively back at him from under the hoodie. He fumbled his hands and let the heavy flashlight hit the floor.

The figure responded by throwing his head back and an unleashing a screeching, garbled cry from a mouth which sounded flooded with blood.

The hollow scream evoked death and pain and would send chills up the arms of anyone who heard it—except Bob, but only because he'd heard the scream before.

The Man went silent, fixing his gaze on Bob, who swallowed hard and yelled the only the thought that came to him. "But...you're dead." His legs gave out. Had Bob not grabbed onto one of the bunks, he would have gone straight to gore-soaked floor.

The sight of the axe scared Bob into action. He straightened himself up and using every ounce of strength left, Bob yanked the bunk down as he stepped away and let the wooden bed crash against the opposite bunks, effectively blocking the aisle. The Man reached the barricade in five huge steps and brought the axe down, hard, pulverizing the bed as the wood splintered under the force until the bunks caved inward.

Bob rushed to the rear windows and tore off the boards. He pushed them aside and climbed out as the Man broke through the barricade and sent wood flying as he took a forceful swing at him. Bob scrambled out the window, the blade narrowly missing him as it came down.

Tyler, Chris, and Jamal sat huddled next to one another behind Kevin's desk in the office cabin. Kevin had grabbed Tyler after witnessing Myer's demise and escorted the trio back to the office. He tried the phone and found, to no one's surprise, no dial tone. The storm or the killer had taken care of that. After the Guide frantically patted himself down several times trying to find the cell phone he'd lost, Kevin paced the cabin, frazzled and unable to think of what to do next, lost without his leader.

"What about our plan to leave?" Jamal whispered, keeping their eyes glued on the two front windows, terrified if they drifted away for a second, they would come back to find the Man standing there.

"Kevin?" Tyler stood up, addressing him. "You have a car, don't you? Can't we leave?"

"We don't keep our cars here in case Journeyers try to steal them."

"Understandable when you're holding people against their will." Tyler waved his hands before Kevin countered. "How do you get to and from camp then? What about supplies? There has to be a way out of here."

"I think we should wait for Bob." Kevin bit at his fingernails and avoided looking at Tyler and the others as he continued around the cabin in a stupor. He'd come up behind Tyler in time to see Myer's head being popped like a stubborn pimple and Tyler noticed the Guide hadn't seemed right since.

"Bob could be dead, and we need to fucking get out of here."

"Language," Kevin snapped as he tried to decide what to do, the struggle evident all over his pained face. "We really should wait for Bob."

"Again, that dude is probably dead," Tyler repeated, but Kevin refused to give up hope on his director. "Kevin," Tyler called out, trying to wrangle the Guide's attention to him. "How do you get to and from camp?"

"There's a bus hidden out by the Hut." His

eyes remained fixed on the door, waiting for Bob.

"Wonderous. Let's get the hell out of here then. Where are the keys?"

Kevin eyes were glassy and vacant, the eyes of a man about to lose what little grip he had left. He laughed before he spoke. "I don't have them."

"Well, who the fuck does?"

☠

The nondescript key to the bus swung on Bob's keyring, jangling from the carabiner attached to his belt loop as he burst into the mess hall, out of breath and terrified. He secured the door by a wooden beam hinged to its right side. Once in place, he put his head up against the door and felt his hot breath slapping back against him from the wood. That scream, the horrible throaty scream, rang in his ears.

"It can't be him, *he's* dead." Bob spoke to the wood, half hoping the door would tell him he was right. When the wood remained silent, Bob pulled his head away and spun around into mess hall to find the room appeared as it had the summer of '95 when he first attended the camp. Memories were like small lakes within his mind, and Bob leaned too far over the side of his darkest one: The mess hall had been filled to the brim with Journeyers and Guides. The plastic tables weren't yet cracked and peeling or vandalized by names scratched into the top. The long picnic tables and their benches hadn't yet begun to splinter and warp. And there amongst the full house and all the noise was Bob, fifteen, fresh-faced, and sitting in the same spot he'd sat earlier for dinner with Karen next to him

He recalled the day of his memory, the one where milk had shot out of Karen's nose and hosed down the lunch tray in front of her. Bob missed whatever joke caused her laughter, preoccupied by a new arrival. Unobserved by everyone else, except for him, the new boy stood in the open doorway with the sunlight bathing him in a shimmery golden aura. Bob's heart skipped. He couldn't pull his eyes off the boy who appeared to have walked off the cover of one of the *Teen Beat* magazines Bob kept secretly stashed under his mattress.

For the briefest of moments, Bob believed teen heartthrob Jonathan Brandis had entered, a daydream he shamefully entertained more than once. The brief illusion however was created by the similar and popular haircut of the time; the boy's thick sun-kissed golden-brown hair parted down the center and curtained up in the front by two symmetrical arches, falling softly back down against his forehead. His bright-blue eyes and big smile didn't help dispel the illusion either.

Room at your table? Bob swore Lucas's deep voice rang in his ears all over again. He had walked up to their table without looking for another place to sit and asked if he could join them. Bob agreed, for he'd never seen a boy so cinematically handsome walking around in real life. When Lucas sat next to him despite the empty chair next to Karen, his heart swooned.

Slapping his hands hard on the table, Bob wrenched himself away from the past. Frankly, none of what had occurred that day, or the days after, were worth remembering. Standing up, he called out for Karen; was she there? If so, he wondered why she'd not commented on his dramatic entrance? When he received no immediate answer, Bob got up and checked the kitchen.

Frozen in the doorway, he forced his hand once again over his mouth, fighting another rising tide of vomit; ham and bean soup had not been the best dinner choice. Karen's body laid splayed out on the broken kitchen island, torso forcefully ripped open like a messy back-alley autopsy, her organs and rib cage all on full display. Bob wondered how many more horrible sights he'd have to endure before the night ended, when the axe connected with the mess hall door in a loud crash. Scanning the kitchen for anything that worked as a weapon, Bob pushed opened the rear door, ready to run, when the pantry to the left of him caught his eye—a hiding place.

Leaving the rear door open, Bob knocked over some of the pots stacked on a rack and made a scene that mimicked him fleeing the mess hall in a hurry before he squeezed himself awkwardly into a half-foot open space in the pantry. The sounds of him shuffling, sucking in his stomach, and trying to get as far from the slats as possible were covered by the axe's final blow. The Man's hand reached through the hole and flipped up the barricade.

The front door swung open, and no sounds followed until tables began being flipped over, accompanied by the axe tearing into the benches. Bob held his breath and kept his eyes focused on the slats of the pantry door as the Man, whom he didn't believe to be Lucas even if the scream had sounded the same, stormed into the kitchen. The open rear door and the pots still rattling on the floor worked in making believe his prey had fled. The Man's hand balled into a fist, and he threw his head back as he let out another howl that made Bob's blood run cold.

Bob clamped his eyes shut and waited. If he were found, he hoped his death would be quick and painless. The Man took the axe to the cabinets, to the fridge, the stove, and the frustrated swings gave way to a few wet slaps, which suggested the axe found Karen's body before going silent.

He waited a few more minutes, holding his breath, rattling off prayers silently, before he exited the pantry, avoiding Karen's body. There were not many people Bob cared for in this world, but she topped the list. His heart broke seeing her laid out like nothing more than some gruesome prop in some haunted house. He resisted the urge to reach out and touch her to say goodbye. "I'm so sorry," he whispered along with more prayers for her soul before he ran into the night, unsure what to do next. He didn't understand or believe someone he'd witnessed die twenty-five years prior was walking around his camp.

☠

The hooded killer stormed past the windows of the office. Jamal, Chris, and Tyler remained crouched behind Kevin's desk, their eyes level with the desktop as they saw the killer pass by the front windows. They ducked down and hoped to hell the killer hadn't see them. Kevin remained quiet, having retreated behind Bob's desk under the large portrait of Jesus, mumbling prayer after prayer.

Tyler, scared as hell and trying to hold himself together, worked through what they would need to do next; find Bob—who Ty believed was dead—and get the key to the bus. With Chris's hand still in his, he squeezed Ty's every so often. Tyler wasn't sure if this was meant to reassure him or if Chris merely comforted himself. Either way, the connection made him feel centered. If they got out of their situation, he wanted more time with Chris. Everything hinged on that *if*.

Searching for the key and trying to get to the bus meant running all over camp until they found Bob's remains, and all while they dodged a killer whose motives remained unknown. The thought made Tyler wince. The memory of Myer's death refused to stop screening in the cinema within his head. But the killer hadn't come for them next and that confused Tyler. He couldn't determine what the killer wanted, the Guides? Them? Or was he hell-bent on getting everyone?

"I don't want to die here," Chris said, breaking Tyler's concentration and the silence.

"We're not going to," he assured him, slipping his free hand into Jamal's creating a chain as he spoke. "We're getting out of here." Releasing them, he stayed crouched as he moved toward where Kevin squatted. The Guide had begun banging his head rhythmically against the wall. "Look, dude, I get Bob's your exalted leader or whatever, but we're going to die if we stay here. Are you going to help us or not?"

Ty hoped Kevin knew he was right, and that there were no options. The Guide nodded softly with his vacant stare, before adding, "what can I do?"

"We need to the key, and once we have it, we're hauling our asses out of here. Is the bus ready? Do we need gas or anything like that? We don't need any more surprises."

"It's good to go. We took the bus out before y'all arrived, and there's a can of gas too." The formation of a plan seemed to help stop Kevin from diving fully over the brink, and he stood up shakily, his eyes glued on the window.

Tyler turned to the others and motioned for them to stand up. "We need the key to the bus. Chances are Bob's dead by now, so we'll need to split up and find his body." He raised his hands, knowing on cue the rest of them were about to protest. "No arguing. This is the fastest, quietest way. A big group of us running around here is an easy target. Let's start with the places where we *haven't* already found a dead body. And we need to be as quiet as possible."

"You saw what that Psycho Saltine did to Myer." Jamal's head shook in a defiant display. They would not be running around no camp, no ma'am.

"If there's only the one key, we've no choice in this. I don't want to go out there either, but we've got to find Bob's body. And we—" Tyler stopped as a disheveled Bob burst into the cabin and closed and locked the door behind him. At the sight of his leader alive and well, Kevin perked up and started ordering the others around as if trying to show he'd been in control the whole time.

"Are you okay?" Bob asked them all as he backed away from the door, nervously looking out the window.

"What is going on out there?" Kevin asked.

"I don't know," Bob replied in an annoyed tone as he moved past him to try the phone on his desk. "I'm guessing you've tried this?"

"Doesn't work." Tyler pushed his way past Kevin. "We need the key to the bus so we can get the fuck out of here. Where is it?"

Bob shot a foul glance over at Kevin, and Tyler knew he had learned something he shouldn't have. "I'm not giving you anything, go sit down."

Tyler positioned himself directly in Bob's way, as far into his face as possible. "I'm not sitting down. I'm not shutting up. I'm leaving your shitty fucking camp. Hand over the key."

Bob held onto the receiver of the phone to call for help, but Tyler did not give the camp director a moment to catch his bearings. He hounded him with question after question about where he'd been and what he'd seen until Bob dropped the receiver and shouted for him to stop. "Give me a dang moment."

"No," Tyler snapped back. "Don't you know what it is going on out there in your camp?"

"Stop pestering me and sit down." Bob trudged away to the other side of the room where an unrelenting Tyler followed.

"Well, you can stay and figure this shit out if you want, but us, we're leaving. The key." Tyler thrust his hand out, prodding Bob, demanding his palm be filled. Tyler noticed Bob averted his eyes, as if in his empty palm Bob had seen something that made him cringe.

"Sit down," Bob demanded. The fight to regain his composure was a struggle he was failing at.

"Give him the damn key," Chris added as he and Jamal stood up.

"Stop talking so loud," Bob shouted. "Do you want Lucas to hear us?" He stopped and slapped his hand over his mouth. Bob darted his eyes away from the curious stares of the people around him to random spots on the floor and ceiling.

Tyler stood there stuck on the fact a name had been said. He'd not referred to their assailant with some random term like "killer" or "stranger" but an actual name. "Who the hell is Lucas?"

"Who?" Bob sounded like an owl as he tried to play off his slip and shook his head, acting as if he did not know anyone by that name, except he failed at being convincing. "I found Karen dead."

"Yeah, and?" Another dead body failed to qualify as breaking news at this point. "Craig and Lisa are dead in the restrooms, your point? Who the fuck is Lucas?" Tyler asked again.

"Language," Bob chided, still refusing to answer.

"Do you know something about what's going on here, Bob?" Kevin hesitantly spoke up, not wanting to question his boss but needing to know as well. "Why won't you tell us what you know?"

"Because, I don't know anything," Bob insisted, lowering his head to dodge their questioning eyes.

"Well, I think you do," Tyler asserted. "And it's time you start talking."

"I don't answer to you, little boy." Bob was quick to dismiss Tyler's demand. "Last I checked, I'm the adult here. I'm in charge."

"You're in charge of dick, and we're tired of

this. There is someone out there killing people, *your* people, and you clearly know something about who it is." Tyler knew he was right; Bob hadn't spit out some name randomly. "Who the hell is Lucas?" he asked again.

"It doesn't matter. It can't be him anyway. He's dead. And dead people do not come back to life."

"Ahem," Tyler cleared his throat loudly while pointing to the gratuitously large painting of Jesus hanging on the wall.

Bob's exasperated face showed he'd dealt with enough for one evening and had zero energy left for another religious debate. He ignored Tyler, only addressing Kevin. "We need to find a way to call the sheriff and get someone out here to help us."

"Hey." Tyler wouldn't accept being dismissed, positioning himself in front of Bob. "We aren't done talking, asshole."

"Oh, I believe we are." Bob looked over his head toward Kevin. "Will you please assist me in getting our Journeyers somewhere safe?"

Tyler waited a moment, and when Kevin didn't immediately move to grab him as had happened earlier that night, he knew Kevin wanted the same thing as him—answers.

"We aren't going anywhere, *Bob*." Ty smirked as he dragged out the syllables in Bob's name rudely. Ty didn't see the camp director raise his arms until the man's chubby hands were on his shoulders, shoving him away.

"Shut your mouth. I'm sick of hearing your voice," Bob shouted.

Tyler unsteadily remained on his feet. Before

he could think of what to do or say next, Chris raced past him and grabbed Bob by his collar. Chris balled his free hand into a fist, raised it, and held it level with Bob's face. "Talk, or I start pounding until you personally meet that Jesus dude you got a hard-on for."

Bob smacked at the hands holding him, but Chris was taller and more muscular. "Get your hands off me, you–"

"You *what*?" Chris asked through clenched teeth, tightening his grip.

Tyler felt the butterflies in his stomach again. The act of someone coming to his defense was a first for him, and despite the tense surroundings, he swooned before jumping back into the fray.

"Yeah, what is he exactly?" Tyler stepped up, eyeing Bob over Chris's broad shoulder.

Bob stammered, unwilling to finish his thought.

Chris growled and pulled Bob closer to him. "Yeah, that's what I thought, you little bitch."

Tyler's smile filled his face as he leaned over Chris's shoulder. "It's time to start talking."

☠

Bob sat in his leather rocking desk chair facing out from the corner of the office he'd been forced into. Four sets of eyes stared at him, each demanding he spill his guts. He scowled at them, including Kevin, who had stood by doing nothing as he was jostled around like a doll by one of his own Journeyers. He sat silently as long as he could. His eyes stayed on Chris, who kept punching his right fist into his palm. The taunting smack of the punch got louder with every hit, and as the only noise in the room, it became unbearable.

"Fine," Bob hissed, angered he couldn't run from his past anymore. "When I came to this camp in '95, there was another young man here named Lucas."

Bob relayed to them a heavily edited story, painting Lucas as a mouthy rebel, who moved through Horizons like an oversexed tiger on the prowl, unabashedly charming his fellow male Journeyers and Guides. Those actions earned Lucas more time in the Hut than anyone before or since in the camp's history. Every day he'd fought against the Guides and the therapy, cursed Horizons and what they did there, and caused scenes whenever he could. Exactly as Tyler had done during First Night.

"I avoided him the entire time. After a few weeks though, he randomly asked me to meet him behind our cabin one evening. I didn't want to, so I said no. But I heard noises and snuck out to see what they were. That's when I saw Lucas being led away by the two Guides. So, I followed them."

The truth was far more salacious; Bob and Lucas had already snuck off more than once to enjoy each other's bodies. After each time, Bob would spend the next day in a guilty haze, torn between wanting to be with Lucas but needing to complete his *Journey*. He'd relented, knowing no matter how hard he'd fought, meeting Lucas would have been unavoidable, and the shame spiral would grip him again. He'd enjoyed the time with Lucas, but once over, Bob would fall to his knees, making multiple promises to himself and God nothing would happen again. But everywhere he went on that last day, he bumped into Lucas, who flashed him that killer smile and gave him a wink. And Bob would again lose any thoughts of resisting.

After being reprimanded for misconduct, Lucas created a huge scene. Many had witnessed him being escorted out of the camp director's office in a screaming fit, vowing to name names and how people would be sorry. Bob worried the rest of the day about whose names Lucas threatened to spill. When Lucas hadn't showed for their appointed meeting time, Bob went looking. He found him with two senior Guides, Rick and Dale, giggling and laughing as they led Lucas away from the sleeper cabin, all three of them playfully touching one another. Jealousy motivated Bob, but in the edited story he relayed, curiosity is what made him follow the trio.

They went to the end of Salvation Trail, and Bob found the area around the large sycamore prepped for their rendezvous; a small fire burned by a spread blanket, and candles were lit around the picnic. Bob found a spot in the bushes a few yards away that hid him from view, but still allowed him to see everything.

There were no lies about the next part he conveyed to them, all of which was horrifyingly real. They laughed and stripped, freely touching one another, and to the casual observer, they were having a damn good time. But when Lucas got fully naked and wasn't looking directly at the Guides, their expressions changed into looks of disgust. To Lucas's face, they played the loathing off and avoided his grabby hands by playfully pushing him around like they wanted to wrestle before beginning their sex-capades, until they backed him up against the tree.

Rick kept him there by kissing him, which left Dale free to take Lucas's left arm and secure a rope around his wrist before switching places. Rick stepped away and looped Lucas's right wrist through the long rope's other end before it snapped taught against the tree. Lucas joked he liked things rough, and for a minute, Bob thought a live-action porno was about to begin. His pants stiffened up as his shame grew.

Dale backed away from Lucas, wiping the spit off his lips, visibly appalled. He began to belt out the Lord's Prayer as Rick retrieved a stolen knife from the mess hall obscured under the blanket. Lucas demanded they stop, but not one to sweet talk his captors, he called them pricks and assholes. Rick traced his long fingers along Lucas's full lips before sliding them into his mouth. He struggled, and Lucas tried to bite at the digits to no avail. Rick finally pinched his slippery tongue between his fingers and pulled it out. Bob closed his eyes when the knife was raised, but nothing blocked out the muffled screaming that followed. When he stomached the idea to look again, it was in time to see Rick pull the severed end of Lucas's tongue away from his mouth. He waved it in the air in front of Lucas before tossing the tongue over his shoulder and onto the hot fire where it started sizzling.

"I didn't want to look, but I couldn't turn away." Bob swallowed hard, hating being forced to continue recounting the worst night of his life.

Dale approached Lucas next with a larger

hunting knife in his hand. "God's work must be finished." The Guide said as he grabbed Lucas's crotch and stretched out his flaccid penis. Lucas tried to scream, but only whimpers and the blood that flooded his mouth came out.

Dale stroked Lucas's penis as he spoke. "You will not derail us from our *Journey* heathen. God forgives your sickness, but let this be your penance." The Guide made the sign of the cross before bringing the knife down and sawing through Lucas's thick appendage. Once separated, he gazed at the limp phallus for a moment before tossing the penis into the fire where it burnt up next to the charred tongue.

"I didn't stay to see what happened next," Bob lied, feeling he had told them enough already. "If they'd do that to him, what would they do to me for bearing witness? I didn't see what else, if anything, they did. I ran to camp and got into my bunk before anyone knew I'd gone. Everyone believed Lucas had run away. And I figured the ordeal would be over. I went out to the tree the next day, and I don't know if they did something with the body, or if...animals got him, but Lucas wasn't there." Bob looked up from the wood floor he'd stared at during the story to see the shocked faces of his audience for the first time, a quartet of disbelieving, horrified looks stared back at him.

☠

Tyler glanced over to the others and saw everyone's appalled face matched his own, their mouths dropped nearly to the floor as they tried to understand the story they'd been told.

"They cut off his dick?" Jamal asked shocked. "I called this shit from the jump—white-people nonsense."

"It's an antiquated church practice for curing homosexuality," Bob explained, as if that alone justified the horrific act he'd recounted to them.

"But you didn't say anything." Tyler glared at Bob and made sure the camp director knew how disgusted he was. "You let those guys get away?"

"I was fifteen, Tyler. I'd seen something beyond awful, and it scared me. My only thought was getting to where I'd be safe," Bob said. "I couldn't say anything, I'd have been questioned as to why I was out of bed. And that would have ended my *Journey*. I didn't do anything wrong here, okay. I was a kid."

As Bob spoke, pieces of a puzzle began to fit for Tyler. "Bob, when did you take over this place?"

"Officially, four months ago is when I became camp director."

"And how many Journeyers have gone missing since you took over?"

"How dare you!" Bob bellowed furiously at Tyler. "I do not appreciate the insinuation. I've overseen over a dozen cycles and haven't lost one Journeyer during that time."

He didn't understand that the question Tyler asked hadn't been an attack against him, but Kevin did. "The Guides." The revelation came out the moment the realization had sunk in for Kevin. "We haven't lost any Journeyers, but five Guides have gone missing in the past couple of weeks.

"They're not lost. They're dead. I found them in one of the unused cabins."

"Do you think it's this Lucas person?" Jamal asked. Tyler was lost in his head, putting the pieces together, and didn't immediately answer.

"Can't be him," Bob snarled in an exhausted tone. "He is dead."

"Well, Hunty, someone out here cutting people the fuck up, and if it ain't yo' dead boyfriend doing it boo-boo, then who?" Jamal snapped their fingers loudly then covered their hand.

Jamal waited for an answer, but Tyler didn't give Bob the chance. "I don't think he wants to kill us."

"Well, that's a relief," Bob exhaled.

"Oh, not you, you piece of shit. I'm 99 percent sure he's here to off *your* ass, but I don't think Lucas is after us. Not when all the victims so far have been Guides."

"Myer wasn't a Guide," Kevin added, hopeful that fact would be enough to dispel Tyler's theory and put him back in the safe category.

"That *young man*"—Tyler opted to not speak ill of the deceased Myer—"was being hella homophobic at the time of his demise. And I'm theorizing here, but I don't think this guy cares for that kind of talk. I might be wrong, but I stood right there, and if he wanted too, he could have killed me."

"Why didn't he?" Bob asked snidely, and Ty knew he was wondering why he lost a good one like Myer.

"I'm pretty sure it's because I wasn't the one who left him tied to a fucking tree."

Bob moved to another corner of the office, but the switch did nothing to ease the tension starting to grow atop their mass fear. "Listen to me all of you; people *do not* come back from the dead and go on murderous rampages."

Jamal whipped their head toward Bob. "Girl, that's the plot of *Friday the 13th* parts six through eleven."

"I'm done with this conversation." Fed up, Bob punched the wall in a rage. "All of you need to shut your filthy queer mouths. Do you understand me? I don't care what is going on out there. In here, you are still under my supervision. And I will–"

Bob didn't finish. A fist connected with his face, interrupting him. One thrown by a teenage boy. Tyler's punch carried enough fiery force behind it, Bob fell to the floor on his ass.

Tyler hadn't expected to punch him, but he'd thrown his balled fist out in front of him before he realized he'd even moved. He stood over a quivering Bob. "You self-righteous cunt. Where the fuck do you get off calling us filthy? I don't think so asshole, not when you're the fucking predator here. That's all you do, isn't it Bob? Prey on the confused and weak? Which I find genuinely ironic considering they're only confused to begin with because of you holier-than-thou, better-living-through-Jesus asshats.

"Tell me, you self-hating piece of shit, how many people have come here only to leave more fucked up? How much unnecessary pain have you caused my queer sisters and brothers? You don't like being gay, that's your own fucking problem. But you don't get to go out into the world and make other queer people feel terrible about who they are.

"And you have the fucking audacity to pull this shit in God's name. Laughable, sir. I don't think *She'd* have anything to do with this place. And I know you don't give a shit about any of what I'm saying—you're too far up Jesus's robes to hear any other side of the issue."

Tyler quit berating him. What was the point anymore? Bob remained on the floor broken, sore, and scared.

"Someone is out there killing your Guides, and he may or may not be the dead boy from your story, but the fact is it's *someone*. And they clearly do not like what goes down in this place. They're here because of you, Bob." Tyler's eyes burned out and onto the sullen Bob. "I'm not the type to wish ill on anyone, but with all the love I have in my heart—I hope you burn in hell for what you've allowed to continue here."

Bob let Tyler finish, holding his chin and unable to find the words to retaliate. Or find the strength to move when Tyler dove down and snatched the keyring from off his belt loop and flipped through the dull ring of flat keys until he landed on a thick black fob.

"Every part of me wants to leave you here for him." Tyler extended his hand, offering to help Bob off the floor. "But that would make me like you, and that's so not my vibe. We're leaving this place together so you can face the fucking cops for what you've done."

Bob smacked away Tyler's hand and stood with venom in his eyes and on the tip of his tongue, but none of the will to act upon it. He moved as far from Tyler as their close quarters would allow and nearer to Kevin, who remained quiet in the corner and had inched away from Bob, disillusioned with his mentor.

"We get to the bus, and we get the fuck out of here." Tyler held up the key in his hand before turning to Bob. "And you're leading the way."

☠

Crouching as low as they could, the group made a beeline to the bus, going behind the office and down past the Guides' cabin before venturing onto an overgrown path into the woods. Instead of going straight to the Hut, Bob veered off on an unmarked trail to the left, his flashlight leading the way. After a few hundred feet, the hood of the midlength yellow bus peeked out at them from the camouflaged canvas cover.

Tyler scanned the area around them as they pulled the cover off. Their walk had not been quiet, and yet there was no sign of Lucas anywhere, and that worried him. Had he intentionally let them get to the bus? Tyler's mind reeled with the possibilities of what Lucas could be doing out there, where he was hiding, and what was in store for them? Ty ushered Chris and Jamal onto the bus, remaining outside, still watching the trees, and certain Lucas allowed them to get as far as they had. Bob followed them, shooting a sour look as he passed Tyler, who still held the bus key in his hand. Ty waited for Kevin to get on as well, but the Guide stopped.

"There is an extra gas can around one of these trees. We need it...in case. Town is a longways away." Kevin checked around the bus making sure the area appeared clear. "When you see me coming back"—he pointed off to the trees past the rear of the bus—"start the engine, and as soon as I'm on, you floor this thing."

"Split up now?" Tyler questioned, unable to shake the feeling he'd led them all into a trap. "He let us get this far. He's waiting for his moment. You need to stay, to drive this thing."

Kevin shook his head. "It's too far. I know where the can is, and I'll be quick." He started to dart away but something prevented him, and when he turned back his sorrowful eyes focused on Tyler. "I didn't...it wasn't..." He struggled with his apology, but finally spit the words out. "I'm sorry for hitting you the way I did. I feel awful about it. I'm very sorry Tyler." Tyler knew the admission was difficult for the Guide to make, and he saw the remorse of his actions cresting in Kevin's face as the mean mug he'd kept on permanently began to fade away.

"It's okay," he assured the Guide with a weak smile, forgiving, but not forgetting. "Get back here fast, so we can get out of here." Kevin thanked him and darted off as Tyler climbed into the bus and jumped into the driver seat.

"Excuse me, what do you think you're doing?" Bob asked, annoyed but holding onto the lever which closed the bus door.

"Waiting for Kevin, I don't trust your ass." Ty slid the key into the ignition.

"And if he doesn't come back? Are you going to drive us? You don't know—"

Tyler popped the parking brake, stomped his foot on the clutch, shifted to neutral, and turned the ignition key. He also knew the bus needed a minute to warm up before he pushed the starter. "My aunt drives a school bus asshole." He gloated to an irritated Bob, who huffed and stammered under his breath. Tyler stared out the windshield into the rainy dark night, wondering where Lucas was hiding and why had he let them get to the bus?

☠

Kevin bolted down the length of the bus and around the trees, unable to remember which one they had hidden the half-full five-gallon metal gas container behind. On the third tree, he found the awkward collection of branches. After grabbing the can, Kevin held it against his chest with both hands and tried to remain still. The can's retrieval made a lot more noise than intended. Even the gas in the container sloshed around loudly trying to betray him, as Kevin readied himself for the sprint to the bus, not realizing Lucas remained behind him the entire time, silently waiting.

When the Guide believed his surroundings were safe enough to run to the bus, he turned around and found himself face-to-face with Lucas. The machete in his right hand raised, ready to strike. As the blade swung down at him, Kevin instinctively threw the gas container up to block the blow. Piercing through the metal can as if it were a wet paper towel, the blade missed Kevin's face by a few inches on its exit. Gasoline sprayed all over him as the machete retracted.

Kevin threw the can down, his focus on desperately trying to wipe the stinging gas flooding his eyes. Lucas grabbed Kevin's throat and pushed him against the nearest tree. He drew an extended-reach lighter, the kind with a five-inch metal shaft, from under his bulky layers. The gas blinded Kevin, burning his throat—he'd swallowed a more than generous amount. He called out hoarsely toward the bus, for those onboard to leave.

A sharp pain silenced Kevin's cries as the end of the lighter was forced up through the fleshy bottom of his jaw. It rose into his mouth, shoving his tongue out of the way as the steel tube came to a stop. The click of Lucas's thumb as he rolled the child-safety lock down sent Kevin spinning. His life played out before his eyes; all his many mistakes, his few joys, all ending the moment Lucas mashed the lighter's igniter down.

Within a minute, the gas, which lacquered the interior of Kevin's mouth—the same gas which had splashed over his face like the incoming tide—ignited in a mini-explosion of bluish-white fire before the intensity simmered into deep yellow and red flames.

Situated at the rear of the bus, Jamal and Chris sat ready to send up the alarm on Kevin's return. They did not instantly understand what they had witnessed in the grouping of trees. A quick flash of light had sparked between some of the trunks as if something exploded, and yet, no sound accompanied the sight.

Chris mentioned maybe a tree had caught fire. When Jamal countered his observation by pointing out the burning tree had moved, they both saw how wrong they'd been. Their horrified faces smooshed against the bus window, watching as Kevin, his body engulfed in flames, staggered away from the trees toward them.

The fire consumed Kevin, erupting out of the sockets as his eyes were cooked, flickering out of his mouth as the fire burned an opening in his throat. The Guide stretched his arms, reaching out for the bus, managing a few steps beyond the tree line before collapsing. Chris and Jamal let out screams that shook everyone on the bus, their faces twisted in terror before they turned away as the fire engulfed Kevin completely. He fell to his knees, hands still clawing at the air, begging for more of the rain that only an hour before had been so prominent. Embracing him like a lover he never got to truly have, the fire cascaded down from his head to the rest of his body.

☠

Tyler saw Kevin's burning image fall to the ground in the rearview mirror. His stomach flipped, telling him to go. He pushed the starter, mashed his foot down on the clutch, and threw the vehicle into gear as a machete careened through the front windshield. Pushing himself in the driver's seat as far as he could go, Tyler checked his right where the blade stopped. Hovering inches from his shoulder, the machete lingered in the space between him and Bob, who had ducked and slid down the three stairs in front of the door.

Lucas jumped down onto the hood of the bus from above, grabbed the handle of the machete, and drew it back, letting the metal grind against the thick glass of the windshield. Tyler slid out of the driver's seat when the blade pulled back enough to allow him and followed Bob. As they reached the back of the bus, the machete's blade slid through the rear door's window. The weapon missed Jamal and Chris, stopping one inch from Bob's face—the blade's intended target. Lucas retrieved the machete and before anyone saw him move, his feet stomped along the bus's roof above them.

"Oh shit!" Jamal shrieked loudly. "He is trying to get up in this motherfucker." Jamal started to crawl over the seats to get to the front. "Oh, Lord, let him kill this bitch Bob, so we may escape. Black Jesus, please in heaven hear this unicorn of color's prayer."

Tyler grabbed Bob's shoulders and pushed him into one of the seats as the bus began to rock back and forth. For a minute, no one spoke or moved; some didn't even breathe. Their eyes were like patrol helicopters searching the areas around them. Tyler saw Chris's pale face, his lips trembling, and blew him a kiss. He hoped the gesture would help before he inched his way down the aisle to the back door. Ignoring the broken glass, he wrapped his hand around the red emergency exit handle.

Lucas was all around them. Every few moments, in an unnerving screech of metal, the machete blade cut through the bus's ceiling and shot down like a piston, trying to find its target. They stayed low to the floor until Lucas's entrance into the bus, crashing in through the front windshield, startled everyone. Tyler jumped away from the exit.

The dark figure stood at the far end of the bus, breathing heavily, remaining still as the dead—observing them. From his stance, he appeared poised to attack, taking a moment to size up which of them would be next. Tyler grew nervous, worried his theory of the Guide's being the only victims was wrong.

Rising from his crouched position, Bob weaseled his way behind him and Jamal. "Lucas?" Bob asked, safely behind the other three with all of them trying to inch away as far as they could. "Is that really you?" Lucas raised his machete as Bob threw his hands up defensively. "Please...I need to know if it's you."

The Man stepped forward and pulled the makeshift scarves away from the bottom of his face revealing a mouth where the skin had receded, leaving his pale, discolored gums and his grime-covered teeth exposed. What little skin remained lacked any color and was as dried as balsa wood. He opened his mouth and let the stump of his tongue slide out, making sure Bob saw the maimed organ flicking up and down in the air before he covered himself up.

"That would a be a fucking yes." Tyler reached down and grabbed the emergency exit handle feeling an increased sense of urgency.

"How is this possible?" Bob asked, unable to stop staring at Lucas in disbelief.

Tyler pulled the handle, waited to hear the lock pop before he pushed the door open. He cringed when the acrid smell of Kevin's cooking body rushed in with the gust of air and singed his nostrils. Chris and Jamal were over the seats, pushing past Bob, and off the bus within a moment. But Tyler waited till they were clear before he thought about going, but he stopped. He stood up and sighed at the annoyance of being the better

Person and grabbed Bob by the shoulder.

"I don't understand?" Bob stood stunned. "How?"

"God works in mysterious ways, don't he? Can we go please."

At the sight of Tyler coaxing Bob to leave the bus, Lucas lunged forward, leapt the four rows of seats between them, and grabbed Tyler. Using his other hand, he smacked Bob into the seat next to them with a forceful blow. Tyler struggled against the grip around his throat. He expected his end to come swiftly, but nothing happened.

Lucas stabbed the machete through the seat in front of Bob's, blocking him in, and pulled the hoods of his jackets down to reveal the top part of his head. The skin, gray and decomposing had flashes of white where his skull showed. His withered face was mostly skull and a small smattering of dry, parchment like skin, which fell off in flakes when he moved. Two white orbs remained deep in the recesses of his dark, sunken eye sockets, and those eyes sucked Tyler into them. He lost himself in the milky whites as they pulled him into a void.

Tyler found himself a stranger moving through someone else's vivid memory, like a deceased actor plopped into a modern movie in which he did not belong. Tyler recognized the scene: the night of Lucas's death. The fire Bob described burned as he said, and bloody knives were laid out on the blanket. Lucas hung from the huge tree, but not alone, someone stood in front of him. They were not the Guides who'd committed the violent acts— they had run off—but a young Bob.

The camp director looked nothing like he did currently, appearing small and innocent in front of the giant tree. The young Bob reached his shaky hand outward, hesitating with every inch until finally resting it on Lucas's chest. The blood trickled from Lucas's mouth like a faucet which had been left on, splashing down on his chest and onto Bob's hand, which he snatched away as if the blood burned. It was then Lucas opened his eyes and howled in pain. The scream frightening Bob, who jumped back almost tripping over his feet as he fled down the path past Tyler and out of sight.

He told us he left before they finished. He lied.

Night merged into day in the time Tyler turned around and faced the tree again. The morning sun filtered through the leaves and the clouds. Its light drifted across the embers of the fire and along the tree's massive trunk until softly caressing Lucas's face where he awoke for the last time.

The restraints holding him gave way, and Lucas fell to the ground, weak and wounded. Tyler followed, unable to help or interact. Lucas struggled to his feet but was brought down when the pain in his mutilated crotch proved too much to overcome. He went to scream, but all that emerged from his mouth was a gargle of blood and then a pain drenched moan. Tears poured from Lucas's blue eyes, and every emotion he was feeling hit Tyler like a truck: loneliness filled to the brim with fear, an aching sadness which struck Ty in his own heavy heart, and the one emotion pumping from Lucas like thick, stagnant bile, the one Tyler was overly familiar with—an unrelenting, burning rage.

Disoriented by his surroundings, Lucas found a last bit of strength and rose to his unsteady feet. He wandered a few feet away and remained standing for the briefest of moments before falling and rolling over onto his back as he stared up at the sky. Reaching up for the sun, he pleaded for help. Every thought racing through Lucas's mind in those final moments echoed in Tyler's ears: each name he called out for help, including Bob's, and the heavy silence which fell after each one. No one would be coming to help him. From deep within his soul, Lucas summoned one final roar as the last spark of life vacated his body, echoing across the forest as he cursed the people who hurt him.

Unsure of what would occur next, Tyler dizzily hung on as the world around him sped by like the time-lapse segment of a nature special. The days morphed into the nights, and into days as nature claimed Lucas's decomposing body—after the animals took their piece. The brush stretched out, invasive vines covering him as the vegetation grew up and over the body like a casket on top of which blue and yellow flowers grew. In his earthly tomb Lucas found his last and permanent embrace from the only mother who ever genuinely cared for him.

Remaining in the same spot, Tyler witnessed weeks turn into months, and those spanned into years, and finally into decades until like the clicking spinner in the Game of Life, the images slowed and rested on Lucas's fully green and lush grave. There was an animal moving around in the grass and flowers, and Tyler questioned why the vision stopped before the realization dawned on him:

this is the day he came back.

A hand burst forth from the burial mound, and the fingers flexed, finding life returned to them once again. The hand dug its way out from under the twigs and leaves, and Lucas pulled himself forward. But the Lucas who emerged was not the slim teenage boy left to die, but the tall, commanding figure he would have grown to become. His body was a tapestry of pain, from the old wounds to the newer ones inflicted by hungry animals looking for a snack. Holes riddled his gray, rotted skin. In patches, the decaying, maggot-infested muscles were visible. The decayed figure bent his head to the sky and bawled loudly. Animals fled from around him as the garbled cry ripped through the forest.

Tyler continued to receive the vision behind his eyes, and they showed him the reason for Lucas's return—an image of a gray-haired Chester Barrett dropping the camp's keyring into Bob's open and eager palm. They said their goodbyes, and Chester drove off, waving out the window as he did. Bob remained in the circular drive, jostling the keys up and down in his hand, dancing in place and savoring his accomplishment. Lucas's anger flared at the sight of a happy Bob. Everything went red in the vision, as violent flashes of what happened next assaulted Tyler like a movie unable to be paused. Lucas stole the clothes he draped himself in and stalked the camp and Guides. Five brutal demises played out with no way for Ty to turn away from the stomach-churning horrors until he exhaled loudly and found himself returned to his body.

Disoriented and confused, Tyler's mind raced like an out-of-control Tilt-A-Whirl, whipping around and around. The world, blurry and dizzying, as he returned from his out-of-body experience. Tyler tried to focus on a stationary point but found none as his new beau sprinted away from the bus with Ty slung over his shoulder.

Lucas jumped down after them, and his feet slammed into the ground as he pursued them. Unsure what happened, Ty didn't move as the ground sped by under him. The scent of Kevin's cooking flesh thickened the air, strongest as they ran past the burning body, which crackled and popped as if Kevin were nothing more than a fresh log tossed on the fire. The sounds and foul smell helped bring Ty fully to his senses.

Gripping onto Chris's muscular back, Tyler closed his eyes. The combination of his out-of-body experience and Kevin's smell made him nauseous. When he did steal glances, they were of Lucas who walked at a slow and steady pace, and yet still gained on them. Bob shouted to go a different way, and Chris argued with him but conceded and changed direction. Lucas removed the hunting knife from under his many layers and sent the blade flying in their direction.

Even though the buzzing in Tyler's ears prevented him from clearly hearing Chris and Bob's conversation, he heard the knife's blade cutting through the air clearly as it passed his ear. Tyler's smooth ride became rough as Chris's feet bounced along the ground, dancing around as he struggled to remain upright with his precious cargo. Disoriented, he missed what the commotion was about, but as they rushed forward, Ty saw Jamal fall to the ground, the knife buried deep in their shoulder.

☠

"You tripped Jamal."

Chris seethed as Bob closed the door to the Guides cabin behind them. Chris set a loopy Tyler down in the first chair he found and spun around with his fists up. Bob, unable to lock the door, backed against the wall weakly, holding up his hands in defense.

"The fuck is wrong with you man? I saw you trip them." Chris, angrier than he'd been all night, let his fists hover near his face, shaking from the restraint he displayed.

"We were rushing," Bob stuttered, fighting to find the words to defend himself. "It was dark. I didn't see Jamal; all I saw was Kevin." Bob paused at the thought of his favorite Guide still out there cooking like pot roast.

Tyler's brain slowed down enough he believed getting to his feet would be no problem. The action made another wave of nausea crest and flip his stomach, and he feared he'd be unable to hold his dinner down. "You left him there," Slurring his speech, Tyler pointed his finger drunkenly at Bob. "You left him."

"We'll go back. I thought Lucas wouldn't hurt any of you, that's what *you* said. We were rushing. If anything happened, it was an accident. We can go get Jamal."

"Not Jamal—Lucas." Tyler sensed Lucas's rage rising within him as if still connected. "I saw you."

"What are you talking about?" Bob asked, weary of Chris's twitchy fists.

"You lied to us when you said you'd left before they were done. But you were there the whole time."

"I think you should lie down. It's been a long night."

Chris glanced over his shoulder, and Tyler, wobbly on his legs, moved closer to them. Caring more about him than Bob, Chris moved and gently took Tyler by the shoulders. "He's right, you don't look so good. You're like pale-pale." He moved the sheet-white Tyler back to the chair and set him in it. Tyler refused and tried to get up and go for Bob again.

"I saw what happened." Unsure how to explain what he'd seen and felt while connected with Lucas in his vision. "I stood there at that tree, and you were right in front of him. He woke up screaming for help, and you ran away." He latched his eyes onto Bob's and refused to let him squirm away. "He was alive, and you left him. *You* killed him."

Bob went limp. The truth he'd worked so hard to hide came tumbling out into the blinding light.

"Why'd you lie?" Tyler asked, his pointed tone making it clear he would not ask a second time.

Bob refused to open up and explain more, claiming his reasons were his own, and he would not be judged by anyone other than his creator. His only offering of an explanation, "You wouldn't understand."

"Fucking try me," Tyler snarled, fighting the urge to pummel Bob and feeling like his old self again. "He was alive when you left him. You're an awful fucking person Bob Kendall, and I swear the next time Lucas is here—" Tyler gritted his teeth and gave up. He couldn't finish the thought, no point in vocalizing what he had no intention of following through with. No matter how angry or how easy taking out all his aggression on Bob would be, Ty refused to lower himself. While his moral compass annoyed him, Tyler backed away from Bob, quieting the rage rising inside him. "You owe us an explanation. You owe the dead Guides littering your fucking camp an explanation."

"Babe, I don't get your play here?" Chris moved between Tyler and Bob. "Why are you trying to save this douche? After what he's done, screw him, let Lucas have him. We need to go find Jamal."

Tyler swooned on the inside at being called babe, but there was no time for teenage hormones. "He's allowed this place to keep going, to keep hurting people. Making money off making people miserable. He needs to be held accountable, and he can't do that if he's dead."

"What about Jamal?" Chris, whom Tyler could tell was wrecked with worry over his friend, wanted nothing more to do with Bob. "What if your theory is wrong?"

"It's not," Tyler assured him, unsure how to explain the *knowing* he had since his vision. But he believed Jamal would be okay. "You're going to tell us why you fucking lied," Tyler demanded, focusing his attention back on Bob.

Sour-faced and angered at being forced to confess, Bob cleared his throat and sat on one of the three old, ratty couches that filled the Guide's cabin sitting area. "I loved him," he admitted. But in doing so, he made being in love sound detrimental like some burden to be avoided. And to Bob, love had been. "I loved Lucas from the minute he sat next to me. When I found out he'd been assigned to my cabin, I was happy. And a night later, he snuck into my bunk. I woke up to his lips on mine. His hands on my body and in my pajamas. I didn't stop him. I didn't want him to stop because I loved him. It's one of the only nights with him I still allow myself to think about.

"He told me I made Horizons bearable. That I was the only reason he hadn't run away." Bob's face twitched as he fought to remain emotionless, recounting the actual truth for the first time in twenty years. "Lucas made me feel safer than anyone ever has in my whole life, and I only knew him for a few weeks. Being with him made all my worries go away. I knew there was nothing we couldn't face, nothing we couldn't do as long as we were together. But that was a lie. Lucas couldn't see the truth of our situation—we had no future, not the way he envisioned for us anyway.

"All we would have were those few weeks, and I wanted to spend them getting better, getting back to my God. Not stressing over getting caught. Not spending every day feeling like I was dirty. I was ashamed. My family expected me to come home cured. To be normal. And so did his, but Lucas never cared about that. He never understood what getting better meant to me. There was no place for us to be together in this world or in God's eyes."

Tyler's gaze drifted over to Chris, and they locked, smiling at each other, unable to ignore how the similarities in Bob's story matched their own.

Tyler may have only known Chris one day, but he did not want the growing feeling to come to an end. It wasn't love yet, but may well have been the bud beginning to bloom. And the first time Tyler had experienced feelings on a deeper level than just sexual attraction. While new to him, he knew love wouldn't include leaving Chris tied to a tree. "So, you loved him, but you did that to him?"

"I didn't do that to him," Bob maintained, but his voice was growing weary.

"Then why did you leave him tied to a damn tree and tell no one? Explain it to me slowly. Explain it to me like I'm fucking five." Tyler refused to allow Bob to lie to them anymore.

Bob's voice went low as he admitted defeat and spoke his truth for the first time in twenty-five years. "I watched Rick and Dale leave. They were laughing about what they did while they put their clothes on. Like they'd just seen a funny movie, laughing like it was nothing. I was scared of them, so I stayed hidden until I was certain they'd left. I wanted to run back to camp, hide in my bunk, but...I also wanted to see. I knew with every step toward that tree, it'd be the last time I ever saw him.

"But when I got to it, all I could see was his mangled crotch." Bob squirmed, clamping his eyes closed as he grimaced from the pain of reliving that night's events. "They hadn't cut *it* off cleanly. They'd tore him up. But I wanted to touch him once more." Bob reached out his shaky hand to touch a tree that wasn't there. "The blood though, the blood was still coming out of his mouth." He withdrew his hand to his chest.

"He was so handsome. Even tied up on a tree

and after how ugly they'd left him." Bob opened his tear-filled eyes, his voice catching in his throat. "But he almost derailed my *Journey*.

"I couldn't say no. I don't think it was possible for anyone tell Lucas no. And if he asked me, I would have run off with him. For a minute, I found it impossible to picture a life without him. I almost threw everything away to risk living in sin and depravity because of my crush. I almost forfeited my soul to eternal damnation for Lucas. And when I saw him on that tree, I smiled." The tears held their positions, no longer cleared for release. His face went cold as his composure returned. The vulnerable side of Bob, the hurt and broken Bob, faded away from his face and back into the dark recesses of his mind where he kept them prisoner.

"I smiled because I was *free*. I didn't feel any remorse as I stared at the dead boy tied to a tree. All I could think of was that the Lord had generously answered my prayer. Do you know how rare a truly answered prayer is in this world? How rare it is to be given a clean slate? And the Lord wiped mine clean with one single blood-soaked gift. I turned my head up to the heavens and I thanked God." Bob brought his hands together in prayer position, holding them at his chest. "I thanked him for rescuing me from the temptations. And, you know, that was the moment he woke up and started screaming. Except it was less a scream and more like a creature, howling in pain, but couldn't get the noise to leave its blood-filled mouth.

"So, I ran. And you're right, I didn't tell anyone. I never brought up the incident again. Even when they asked the next day if I'd seen him, I told them no. Because I was—" Bob looked at Tyler and Chris, his face as joyous as a child's on Christmas morning— "happy."

The word floated away from Bob's lips like a balloon released at a party, floating up toward the ceiling. He'd proclaimed his truth: Lucas being killed made him happier than he ever imagined. His body relaxed as, Tyler assumed, a relief he'd not known his entire adult life washed over him.

"I wanted to focus on getting better. I *needed* to get better. He wouldn't have let me complete my *Journey*. He hated this place and everything it stood for then and now. But Horizons means the world to me. This place is my calling. This place is my home. I knew it my first day as sure as I know it now, Horizons is where I belong. And the only thing I wish happened differently was that I'd stayed in my bunk that night. I didn't need to see what they did to him. Why did I have to be there in his final minutes? I shouldn't have had to carry the memory of some dead boy with me my entire life when I didn't do anything to begin with."

"Wow." Tyler stood, dumbfounded, squeezing Chris's hand and wanting nothing more than to open the door and call out into the night for Lucas. But the fear Lucas might carve through them all, if that's what it took to get to Bob, still lingered.

"You're looking at me like I did those awful things—I never hurt him. I was a kid who wanted to get better, nothing else. I didn't do anything wrong."

"What did you mean you were there?" Chris asked, pulling Tyler away from Bob, whose head was in his hands as he rocked and repeated how he'd not done anything wrong.

"Lucas showed me a kind of vision." Ty explained, "I saw the night he died and the day he came back. All the dead Guides, which I mean, kind of gratuitous, but who I am to direct his vision. I don't know why he showed me all these things, but he did."

"I do." Chris caressed Tyler's face softly. "He sees himself in you. I mean you sound like him in Bob's story. I don't think he hurt Jamal on purpose, and I don't believe Jamal is dead either. But we need to look for them...in case. Because what if Lucas gets angry we're helping Bob?" Chris vocalized a valid fear.

"Okay, we'll go look." Tyler agreed, grabbing Chris's hand, happy to not be alone.

"Where's a phone when you need one? We could call them." Chris didn't know what'd made Tyler perk up, grab his face, and plant a huge kiss on him. But excitedly Tyler turned to Bob.

"Bob, where's their cell phones? I didn't have one when I got here, but you told me you confiscated them, so where are theirs?"

Remaining silent, Bob pushed himself up off the couch and moved through the cabin, disappearing into his room. He popped out a moment later with a small grey metal lockbox and stopped before setting the box on the table. He started to laugh as he flicked his finger on the tiny padlock hanging on the outside.

The momentary relief drained away from him when Ty realized the key was on the keyring dangling from the ignition on the bus.

Bob tossed the metal box on the table. "Well,

there is a good chance their batteries are dead anyway."

"Don't you have one? One of the other Guides?" Tyler questioned.

"No, we lead by example here at Horizons," he said haughtily as if the camp's reputation still mattered. "I prefer landlines. Kevin had his phone on him, did any of you see if he called the—" Bob didn't get to finish his thought. The door to the cabin flung open and slammed against the wall as a wounded, bleeding Jamal threw themselves inside.

"A. Unicorn. Is. Injured. Somebody help a bitch. Somebody. Help. A. Bitch." They shouted as Chris jumped to action, scooping Jamal up and getting them into a seat. Chris pressed his hands against Jamal's wound to help stymie the flow of blood from their shoulder.

"We need a first-aid kit," Chris barked.

"You're all right?" Bob questioned, shaken by Jamal's entrance.

"No thanks to you, you salty-ass Saltine, trippin' people to get away from a killer—you a dirty mother-fucka'." Jamal's eyes were wide with anger, staring through Bob before they turned away.

"You're all right though?" Tyler asked. "He didn't—"

Jamal winced while shifting their body to get more comfortable. Their free hand went to their forehead as Jamal let out a soft, but dramatic, moan. "No, he wanted his damn knife back, rude ass coulda asked instead of ripping that shit out of me like I'm a kabob."

"Where the hell is the first-aid kit?" Chris shouted again, clearly worried about the amount of blood oozing out through his and Jamal's fingers despite the pressure they applied.

"I'll get it, it's in the—" Bob was interrupted again as the door at the rear end of the cabin exploded inward in a fury of splintered pieces as Lucas rammed his way in, and before those spinning, shattered fragments of cabin door fell to the floor, Lucas had lurched forward and flung his axe through the cabin. It slammed into the wall an inch away from Bob's petrified face. The camp director shrieked as he jumped back. Wasting no time, he bolted out the door, yelling over his shoulder for the others to follow.

"Where'd the hell he go?" Jamal pointed to the rear of the cabin. And the others saw Lucas had vanished. Tyler and Chris, who'd yet to process everything that had happened in those few short moments, were as confused as Jamal.

"I think we need to go." Tyler wanted out of there and he helped Jamal to their feet.

Without time to find the first-aid kit, Chris stripped off his shirt, wrapped the oversized tee around the wound, secured the shirt in a knot under Jamal's arm, and made sure the bandage was tight.

"Oh, so gratuitous," Jamal exclaimed, fanning themselves at the sight of Chris's chest. "Keep going though," they said playfully through the pain. "Well finally...I see you girls did something right."

"What are you talking about?" Chris asked.

"Ya'll called the cops, didn't ya?" Jamal motioned to the window where lights shined through, painting the cabin in swatches of blue and red.

☠

Through the windshield of the patrol car, Sheriff Rutherford Doyle grew nervous at how dark the camp was as he brought the car to a stop in the circular drive. The storm turned what should have been an easy night into a long, drawn-out headache. Thanks mainly to the power going out to most of South Lake Never, his hands were full dealing with the mess the outage created. His deputies were out in force trying to clean up the best they could. When he'd found himself ready to head home, he remembered Bob and Camp Horizons. Tired and exhausted, he slammed down the phone when he there'd been no answer after his fifth try. Grabbing his hat, he bellowed for the last deputy free to join him.

Doyle liked Bob and truthfully, had no issues with what they did at Horizons. Doyle agreed getting kids on the straight and narrow was indeed God's work. A knot had grown in his stomach since the storm rolled in, and the quietness of the camp made the knot tighten. He patted his pumpkin-sized belly, which stretched his sheriff's uniform to the point his buttons screamed for help. "Don't seem too bad out here. No trees down."

"Where the hell is everyone?" Deputy Sean Vasquez asked, his focus, like Doyle's, was on the three lampposts lining Harmony Lane, which were still on, yet the cabins were all dark.

"Bob would never let *them* leave. No, they're here somewhere." Doyle's hand ran through his unkempt white beard as he scanned the camp for any signs of Bob.

"Sir, don't they brainwash kids out here or something? This place creeps me out." Sean knew exactly what occurred at Horizons, and he didn't care for it, but he also knew the company he was in. Minds weren't as open as one would hope in the South Lake Never P.D.

Doyle erupted in coarse laughter. "Nah, getting them boys good with the Lord isn't brain washin'. It's God's work, what it is. And we need more of that thinking nowadays if you ask me." The sheriff threw open his door. "Damn homos weren't allowed to run around and whine about equality in my day. They were outta sight and outta mind where they belong. Where a whole lot of people belong if you ask me." He mumbled the last part, but the sheriff's feelings about anyone who wasn't vanilla-white superior were well known to the Puerto Rican deputy.

"I bet them queer sissies lost their shit when that storm rolled through." Doyle laughed again as he heaved his overweight frame out of the car and reached in to grab the mic from the dashboard. "Bob Kendall...it's Sheriff Doyle. Everything all right out here? Do you need any assistance?" The sheriff's raspy, three-pack-a-day voice echoed through the quiet camp from the loudspeaker.

Doyle palmed the mic and held onto it, worrying he'd yet to receive a response. Geared up to make another announcement, he stopped when Bob sprinted from between the office and Integrity Cabin's grassy area. Bob's arms flailed wildly as the pudgy camp director struggled to remain on his feet, his face flushed, and his eyes wide with fear as he ran in the direction of the car.

Doyle expected to see someone immediately behind him, but Bob's attacker emerged from in front of the office—appearing out of nowhere—brandishing an axe. There wasn't time for Doyle to question where the figure had come from. The Man took a swing at Bob, who stumbled at the right moment, and the axe missed his face. The weapon sailed over him and slammed into the ground, tearing up a divot and sending a spray of wet soggy dirt and grass into the air. The debris rained down on Bob as he continued onto the driveway, yelling.

"Doyle, he's killing people."

Doyle, with forty-five years of law enforcement experience under his belt, dropped the mic, pulled his firearm from his holster, and raised the gun within five seconds of Bob's panicked cry. But Doyle's speed and accuracy weren't any help. Lucas was in front of the sheriff before a single shot was fired. The axe blade sliced across his torso, and Lucas disappeared into the darkness as fast as he'd appeared.

The figure moved quicker than Doyle expected, so fast he'd not registered what occurred until he peered down at his slick, blood-covered hands. They fumbled over each other as he tried to hold his stomach together, but the wound burst open and his intestines rolled forward. They tumbled out, spilling over his hands, and sliding through his fingers. Doyle fell to the ground with glazed eyes as he held up his own innards, examining them in a state of disbelief before opening his mouth to speak. Nothing came out, and Doyle's eyes rolled back in his head before he toppled over in a heap.

"Freeze, fucker." Deputy Sean jumped from the passenger side of the car, his gun sweeping in all directions as he checked for an assailant who'd somehow vanished. "Show yourself." The demand came more forcefully this time as the deputy spun in a clockwise motion, unaware that like a shark stalking in the darkest waters, Lucas was all around him.

Swinging the gun around again, Sean saw a trio of young men who had run up behind Bob. "Kids, get down," he ordered, pointing the gun away from their raised hands as they ducked, revealing no one behind them. Deputy Sean remained still, waiting for something to move, not realizing Lucas was next to him. The axe blade broke out of the night air with a shiny gleam, came down hot and fast, and cut through the deputy's wrist with near-surgical precision before disappearing into the darkness.

Sean didn't register what had happened until he watched his hand, still gripped around the gun's handle, fall away from his arm, bounce off the hood of the car, and land on the gravel drive. In shock, he held up his cleanly severed stump, and through the spurting jets of blood, Lucas approached him. The deputy fell against the car, slid to the ground, gripping his stump, and closed his eyes.

☠

Tyler, Jamal, and Chris saw Deputy Sean's severed hand land on the ground a few feet from Bob. They watched as Lucas stood over the deputy, but the imposing figure did not move to strike the injured man again. Tyler's gaze pulled toward Bob, who'd grabbed Sean's severed hand. The director pried back the fingers from around the gun's handle and pulled the weapon out of the grip of the still-clenched hand. He aimed the firearm at Lucas and fired. The hooded figure turned his head toward Bob after the first two shots he got off missed.

"I won't let you ruin this place, you sonofabitch," Bob yelled as he fired off several more rounds. Only three hit Lucas, and surprisingly, they sent the ferocious killer to the ground. The gun's recoil proved too much for an untrained Bob, who had lost control and dropped the firearm while fighting to maintain his balance.

"We can go now, boys," he said once steady on his feet, and he urged them to move, waving them toward the patrol car.

"I ain't going nowhere with you, asshole." Jamal spit in Bob's direction, a devious grin on their face. Bob, enraged with the disrespect, hadn't noticed Lucas smoothly rising to his feet, but Jamal had. "Yes," they cheered on quietly, "get that holy-rollin' son-of-a-saltine-bitch."

"You will do as I say," Bob shouted, frustrated like a child who hadn't gotten their way. "Now, get in the damn car!"

"Language," Tyler scolded mockingly, smiling as he too spotted Lucas, who had moved away from the delirious Deputy Sean. The deputy remained situated against the car, sobbing for his lost hand. Lucas snatched Bob by the shirt and lifted the camp director off his feet. He flipped him over and slammed him down onto the hood of the patrol car. Lucas raised his axe high in the air.

Both Chris and Jamal excitedly waited for Bob to get his comeuppance. But Tyler resisted giving into the joy of the moment. If Bob died, no one would learn about the abuses at Camp Horizons, and no one would be held responsible because the truth began and ended with the camp director.

Tyler winced as he spoke, unsure of what he was thinking or doing, but feeling compelled to shout anyway, hoping his words would catch Lucas's attention. "Lucas, please stop." Lucas stalled the axe over a quivering Bob and turned to the trio standing in the light drizzle of rain within the patrol car's headlights. Despite believing they were in no danger from the towering figure, he was still a terrifying sight. His hand remained firmly gripped around the axe's handle. His shoulders rose and fell with his heavy shallow breathing, ready to strike at any minute. But he let Tyler speak.

"I know you want him dead. To rip him apart for all the fuckery he's caused. And he deserves it, for sure. What they did to you—tried to do to us—is unforgivable. But—" Tyler hesitated before continuing. "—that piece of shit needs to live."

Lucas's growl rumbled through the night air. The vibration of it reverbed within their bodies, sending the hair on the arms and neck to stand up. He raised his shoulders and kept them lifted and tense, clearly unhappy with Tyler's words.

Tyler's face remained soft. He kept his tone as smooth as possible. "You hate him. We hate him. I don't think God's fond of his ass right now either. But if he dies, the truth of Horizons goes with him. They'll be no one to answer for what's happened here. They'll close this place, but Horizons will start over somewhere else and this shit will never end.

But if the cops get his ass, this is over. There will be a trial, a whole fucking media circus. There will be outrage, online and in real life, and those who were forced to come here will get a chance to step forward and tell their stories. People think differently now, Lucas, more of them are accepting. They'll be angry about this place and what he's done. And they'll demand someone answer for these crimes—him." Tyler pointed to Bob, who slid off the hood and cowered on the ground by the car.

"I know vengeance is what brought you back tonight, but maybe you're here to save us." Tyler held out his hands, which Jamal and Chris took in theirs. "So you could make sure we were the last people this place hurts. You saved us tonight, Lucas." Chris and Jamal nodded and held up their hands in agreement. "Thank you," Tyler's voice raised up as if to give a celebratory toast at a birthday party. "You're our big brother, our protector, and you've rescued us from heinous monsters of this world. What happened to you wasn't right. It's unfair, and I'm sorry no one knows your truth. You didn't deserve this. I love you Lucas—we love you." And Tyler spoke the truth. Every word honest and sincere without a hint of his normal sarcasm. Lucas's face stayed hidden under the shadows of his hood, and it was impossible to notice if what Tyler said affected him until the tightness in his frame softened. The death grip on the axe lessened.

"Girl," Jamal exclaimed, stretching out the word through the side of their mouth. "Did you just talk down a supernatural-ass spree killer? Impressive."

Tyler threw out a playfully cocky thank-you. He titled his head toward Bob, who remained curled on the ground, and spoke to Lucas. "Killing this pious prick is letting him off easy. What he did to you, to the others, should weigh on his fucking shoulders for the rest of his small, insignificant life."

Bob's face twisted in anger: his intense eyes glared out as his bottom lip quivered.

"He's not weaseling out of this either. We're going to force his ass to confess to *everything*. The truth is long overdue, and people will know what he did here. And your parents will finally know what happened to you."

At the mention of his parents, the axe dropped from Lucas's hand and fell to the ground. Tyler sensed his wave of sadness as he had in the vision. Lucas appeared as a hulking, gore-covered madman, but inside, he was still the sixteen-year-old boy whose life had been cruelly stolen away. Tyler wondered if Lucas's parents had ever inquired about what had happened to their son. Or did they accept the story of him running away and move on with their lives? Tyler confidently believed Michael and Nadine would do the same.

"We want you to be happy now, Lucas. Tell us what you need to move on from this place, and whatever we can help you with, we will."

Lucas remained still and silent with his head lowered, and the impression among them was Tyler's words had succeeded. Believing their night might finally be over, that Lucas was finished, Ty relaxed. Which, of course, is when Bob sprung up behind Lucas with the axe in his chubby hands. Tyler went to warn Lucas, but Bob moved faster.

"God sees you," he screamed, burying the blade into Lucas's back. Lucas spun to counter before the next blow, but Bob refused him the chance. "I. Did. Not." With each blow Bob delivered, every ounce of frustration he'd carried for twenty-five years flowed out of him. "Do. Anything."

Repeating the phrase over and over, he slammed the axe down upon every word, striking Lucas until the blows sent him to the ground and pulverized his chest. Thick black ooze pumped out of his body instead of blood, spraying up and out in all directions, showering Bob as he continued to swing the axe like a man possessed, ignoring Tyler's frantic pleas for him to stop.

Nothing except Bob's own sanctimonious voice could be heard as he insisted to the world he'd not done anything wrong. "I didn't tie him to that tree. I didn't cut *it* off. I didn't do anything."

After the thirtieth or so swing, covered in thick black blood, panting and exhausted, Bob brought the axe down for what he'd deemed would be the final time. Lucas never fought back, nor struggled against the axe. He laid there, letting each blow come as Zen as a monk on fire. But as the weapon made its last descent, Lucas's hand grabbed the wood handle. Bob froze, his pupils went wide, and no matter how hard he tried, the axe would not descend any further. Lucas flung the axe backward with such force Bob couldn't get out of the way. The blunt end rammed into Bob's right cheek, shattering the bones on the side of his face. His face drooped, as he stumbled back, spitting out broken pieces of teeth.

Lucas stood, unphased by any of the attack, despite still leaking the viscous black blood. He rammed his fist into Bob's stomach, pushing through until he reached around the spinal cord. The force caused an eruption of blood to shoot out of the camp director's mouth in a geyser, which showered down over them.

"*Bobby.*" Lucas, with his fist rooted inside Bob, spoke. The voice touching Bob's ears was the identical one he held in his memory from that first golden Wednesday afternoon when Lucas walked into the mess hall and sat next to him. Stunned from the vicious blow which had destroyed his face, the corners of Bob's mouth turned upward into a crooked smile. His heart leaped at hearing his only love's voice once again.

"*God sees you.*"

There was no love left in Lucas's blackened heart as he wrenched the upper half of Bob's body to the left while his free hand whipped up, grabbed him at the neck, and with a steady motion pulled in the opposite direction—ripping Bob in twain. The two halves of his body flew in the swash of red and blue lights. The top half of Bob released all its internal organs with a sickening splat as the body fell to the ground with a hard thud, his waist and legs falling thirty feet in the opposite direction.

Lucas moved to where Bob's top half landed and grabbed the body by its hair. He turned only once to look at the trio, who remained frozen in their spots uncertain what he might do next. He gave them a simple tilt of his head, a thank-you, before he walked off.

Chris and Jamal rushed the patrol car; Chris went for the radio to call for help as Jamal tended to Sean. They took off the deputy's shirt and belt and secured them over the bloody stump in as tight a tourniquet as could be made.

"What happened?" the weary deputy asked.

"O' girl, you survived. I'm proud of you. And ya' know it's one of them things. They tied that one tall-ass honky to a tree and cut his business off and left him to die. So naturally, he brought his trifling ass back from the dead many years later and started killing all these other Saltines off. Honey, I am telling you right here, right now, my cute and sweet Hispanic churro, white-male rage is an epidemic no one is talking about."

Deputy Sean followed along as if nothing Jamal recounted sounded fantastical to him at all. Jamal assumed his reaction was from the shock.

"You know something," Sean spoke only once more as Jamal carefully helped him into the backseat. "I hate this fucking lake." He gave no elaboration on his comment before closing his eyes. Jamal wasn't sure what he'd meant but agreed with him.

Tyler remained in the driveway, his emotions bubbling up as Lucas stalked back into the woods. Both gratitude for being saved and a deep, pitiful sadness floated over Tyler; the latter, not his own, but the feeling had not subsided since being in Lucas's vision. Tyler's hope the camp director would have finally been forced to spill his guts to the police ended with Bob's death. "Goodbye Lucas," he whispered, holding up his hand in a motionless wave.

Lucas stopped once, and when he did, another catalogue of images blasted Tyler's mind as if he'd turned on his iPod, and it was on full volume. When the assault passed, Ty understood what needed to be done. And Lucas resumed his trek, pulling Bob's top half alongside him like a carry-on bag through an airport as they disappeared within the swishes of blue-and-red lights.

☠

Tyler's finger pushed against the Pepsi button on the vending machine, and the mechanical groan was followed by a can popping out with a loud thud, which he found aggressive that late at night. He was already annoyed since he didn't care for Pepsi, and the Coke machine was two floors down, which wasn't happening as he found the act of putting the next dollar bill in taxing enough. Tyler summoned enough energy to push the Hawaiian Punch button for Chris, finding his beau's choice endearing, and when the brightly colored can rolled into the tray, Tyler couldn't help but be enamored with Chris a little more.

After leaving the alcove with the vending machines, he crossed through an empty waiting room. At close to two in the morning, the TV played on mute. The magazines were stacked on the side tables neatly, and the empty chairs were wet with streaks from where they'd been recently wiped cleaned. The stinging smell of disinfectant lingered in the cleaning crew's wake. He enjoyed the thick scent of lemony cleanliness after a gross night running through the woods in the rain, and the copious amounts of blood.

Ty noticed the talking quieted as he passed the nurse's station, their eyes focusing on him, their lips twitching unable to wait until the gossip started up again. Maybe they went silent because of his weary, dirt-stained face or his lone unmotivated shuffling down the hall. Or more likely the splattering of Bob's blood which stained the Camp Horizons shirt he'd yet to change out of. The news *something* occurred at the camp spread through the hospital with the speed of an unchecked virus. Tyler kept his head down, not wanting to make eye contact, not wanting to be drawn into any conversations. But once he moved out of earshot, their hushed tones rose again.

He'd been up since five that morning, and the adrenaline which kept him going most of the day and night had worn off once they rushed Jamal into the emergency room. His ass dragged. His feet ached. He wanted out of the bloody clothes, to be in a hot shower, and some sleep. The manilla folders he'd stuffed in the rear of his pants before the cops arrived scratched the top of his butt while Erin/Lisa's tape recorder weighed down his rear pocket. At one point, he'd been ready to hand everything over to the police—along with truth, as hard as the truth might have been to swallow. When the arrogant detective questioning him and Chris in the waiting room began to get agitated and refused to acknowledge Bob's abuses, Tyler decided against giving them any of the information.

He gave a stunning performance as the dazed, and still-terrified Final Boy, conjuring fake tears acting jittery and nervous as he recounted the story of an abusive conversion camp and of the hooded figure who walked out the woods like a living nightmare, showering Horizons in blood. He told the detective the truth with one omission— Lucas's identity.

The rugged Detective Matthews, who oozed toxic masculinity as easily as one perspires, refused to believe none of them saw their attacker's face during the night's events. Tyler explained more than once the killer's face was covered, which Chris confirmed by giving the same description. Matthews grew frustrated, and now it was too dark to search the woods around the camp thoroughly. By morning, their perpetrator would be long gone. An unacceptable conclusion since Sheriff Doyle counted among the victims. His death made the situation extremely personal for everyone at the police department, and no one would be resting until their fallen commander's killer faced justice.

Matthews made them repeat the events of the day in as much detail as possible, to the shock and horror of the few nurses and late-night ER patients who overheard them in the near-empty waiting room. Urging them to skip the parts about Bob, the camp, and focus only on the topic Matthews cared about—the killer. The realization dawned on him the detective wouldn't be helping them in the way Ty hoped. They wanted a swift closure, a case wrapped up nice and neat so life would return to normal. And they could resume pretending nothing nefarious happened on the daily at Camp Horizons.

When Matthews got heated at their lack of noticing one detail of their attacker, he all but accused them of lying. Tyler shut down the questioning by curtly reminding the flustered detective they were minors who had not committed a crime, stating he and Chris refused to answer any more questions until their parents were present.

Defeated, the detective stormed out of the hospital, screaming into his walkie he wanted everyone back out to Horizons. As the enraged detective continue cursing and yelling on his way out, a patrol car met him at the door. He shouted at the driver as he got in and was driven off. Chris laughed and asked if every interaction with Tyler and an authority figure always ended the same way.

Ty rolled the cold can of Hawaiian Punch in his palm and walked toward Jamal's room, laughing to himself how every interaction he tended to have did usually end with someone storming off in a huff. And no lie, he loved it. The officer seated outside Jamal's door had dozed off, his head rolled back on his neck, his mouth opened wide emitting tiny snores. Their sleeping protection only added to Ty's annoyance with the LNPD since as far as the cop and everyone else knew, there was a killer still after them. Once inside, Tyler pushed the door closed harder than necessary and startled the sleeping officer awake.

The rain picked up again, slapping against the windows behind Jamal's bed. They slept quietly with their shoulder wrapped up in white gauze, stained by the blood, which continued to seep through. There were ten stitches and thankfully no other damage to Jamal's shoulder. Chris pulled his feet down softly from the edge of the bed, muted the already low television, and straightened up as Tyler handed him his drink.

"They wake up yet?" Ty whispered

Chris shook his head. "The nurse said they'd probably be out for the night thanks to the meds. I corrected her on the damn pronouns, twice," Chris said, still agitated the kind nurse could not understand something so simple. "But she left us extra blankets and pillows. And a towel so you can use the shower."

As he moved the pile of blankets and pillows from the chair and was about to kick his feet up, he remembered the manila folders and the recorder. After retrieving them, he set the collection of evidence down on the end of Jamal's bed.

"Is that where you disappeared too before the ambulance came?" Chris asked and guzzled his drink, wiping the red residue off his full lips after each sip. "To get Lisa's tape recorder? What are those files?"

"Those shithead cops aren't going to do a fucking thing for us. What happened tonight will get covered up and forgotten about. They'll pretend the camp never existed. So, I'm going to find the magazine or website Lisa, or whoever she actually was, worked for. I'll give them the recorder and our story, and everyone will know what happened at that camp."

"Our parents are going to be here soon, aren't they?" Chris turned solemn, tossing his already empty can into the trash. Their parents were notified by the detective and on their way.

"Don't worry about them." The same concern crept into Tyler as well, but he wasn't going to let their impending arrival deter any plans. "We're almost eighteen. They can't keep us apart for long.

Plus, I'm thinking after all this near-death shit we went through, they might be a bit more chill—hopefully." An assumption he put no faith in. "We'll figure things out, babe." Tyler moved around the bed to Chris. "I know I'm not ready to lose you, so we're going to make this work." He sealed his assurances they would be all right with a series of passionate kisses.

"If ya'll sneak-ass Saltines thinkin' you gonna ditch-a-bitch, you best think again," a weak but still sassy Jamal proclaimed. They sat up in bed, wincing from the tightness in their shoulder. "Someone needs to stay and help me deal with all the post-traumatic stress I'm fixin' to have after all this white nonsense. I'm staying with y'all for the long haul. Oh, that's right, hunty. Third. Wheel. Officially. Girls, start feeling it. Start living it." Jamal went to clap their hands to give their words some panache, but the pain and the drugs prevented any flourishes. "Please get me up out of this honky-ass town first."

"Of course, and we're staying together." Chris gently took Jamal's hand and grabbed Ty by the wrist to bring him closer. All three placed their hands together. "No one is splitting us up."

"Girl, that's real moving and all, but what about Lucas?" Jamal asked once they'd broken their tender moment, and Tyler moved away to grab his towel. "Is he going to be stuck out in those woods, cutting up homophobes for all eternity?"

"I think if we don't help him, he will be." Tyler started to explain. "Now, I've not figured all the details out yet, but I think I know what we can do. He saved us, so we're going to try to save him."

Tyler picked up the two folders, which contained the personal information for two of Camp Horizons' ex-Guides.

☠ Two Months Later ☠

The ripped and tattered ends of the yellow police tape hung off nearly every tree and post along the driveway of Camp Horizons, fluttering in the wind and refusing to leave like the last annoying drunk person at a party. They all conveyed the same notion: shit went down here, so stay far away. The silence of the sunny, cloudless afternoon was disturbed by the obnoxious roar of a supped-up Hemi engine as a black Challenger roared to a stop in the circular driveway.

In the distance behind the trees, Lucas waited. His hands lowered to his sides, the machete extending out from in front of his crotch, the makeshift replacement for an appendage he no longer had. The hard blade trembled in his hand, excited and reeved up, ready to be unleashed.

Rick Mallis, no longer the thin, fit, black-haired beauty he'd been that night in '95 when he cut off Lucas's tongue, stepped out from the passenger side, hiding his hangover behind dark designer sunglasses and a shitty attitude. The noise of the car door slamming echoed through the quiet camp. "Jesus," he proclaimed, annoyed as he clutched at a string of imaginary pearls around his neck. "Dale, why of all the places in this shit state are we here?" He had not seen nor talked to Dale Palmer in four months after spending twenty destructive years married to him.

Dale scrunched his round face at the sight of the dilapidated camp. "If you weren't sauced already, you'd remember what I told you last night."

"Don't fucking start," Rick snarled, ready to get into a fight after hours in a silent car ride with his ex. He did not want to spend a moment longer at Camp Horizons then necessary. Memories were hiding around every corner. The unpleasant ones outnumbered the good however, and they were ready to spring out and bite him.

Dale knew his only control when it came to Rick was in his reactions, and he'd spent the last seven years of their marriage practicing nonreaction. "We got a letter from an attorney stating we were left the camp by a Robert Kendall. I don't know him, but apparently, he was here when we were. I don't remember, but I'd rather not recall anything from this damn place."

"Wasn't he that kind of pudgy kid infatuated with—" Rick stopped himself before saying the name and kicked at the gravel, not noticing a few of its pieces were stained with the blood of the same person they were discussing. Dale's intense green-eyed gaze burned into Rick's skin for skirting dangerously close to the one topic never discussed—that night. The night which they'd erased from their memory. A night, twenty years and seventeen psychiatrists had explained away as cult behavior, and not really their fault.

"Sorry," Rick apologized as he scanned the cabins, seeing them not as the dilapidated messes they were, but as the sparkling gems they had been in their heyday. Unable to resist eliciting the past, he pointed to the right side of the mess hall. "Our first kiss happened right over there, remember? Best kiss of my life actually." He hoped Dale still held onto the good times at least and not the awful way their marriage ended.

"I already told you I don't want to be here. I don't want to go down memory lane in this fucking place. If this camp is ours now, we're selling this shithole as quickly as possible for whatever money we can get, and we're never bringing Horizons up again." Dale paced around the car, looking down the drive for any sign of a vehicle coming to join them. He ignored Rick's best kiss comment, not wanting to fall into a trap or be forced into memories he had no intention of revisiting.

"Shouldn't someone meet us at least? I mean—rude." The beautiful day made Horizons and Lake Never deceivingly pretty.

"The lawyer," Dale struggled to recall the name on the certified letter he'd received. "A Tyler-something, is meeting us here at two." Dale checked his watch—two twenty-two.

"Well, bitch is late," Rick commented with a bit of vocal fry to his voice, which drove Dale nuts. "A little rude if you ask me." He secretly hoped Horizons being left to them was a hoax simply so he could see Dale's chubby cheeks puff up like a blowfish and get beet red from being angry. Harmony Lane stretched out in front of him, and without trying, he recalled his days there as a Journeyer and then as a Guide. Though he didn't allow his memory to stray far, preferring to keep his thoughts solely on his Journeyer days. Rick stepped forward ready to go explore.

"I wonder if our old cabin is—"

"Stop," Dale insisted, seeing the figure standing in front of them that Rick hadn't noticed. He grabbed Rick's upper arm and pulled him back on his feet.

"Jesus, Dale, what the actual fuck." Furious at the intrusive move, Rick snatched his arm away and fought to keep his balance under the shifting gravel.

"Look."

Rick ignored him as he rubbed his upper arm and checked the red mark lingering from Dale's intense grip. "I swear if you bruised me, I'm going—"

"Shut up." Dale's voice trembled. Noticing the change in his tone, Rick's gaze drifted from his arm back toward Harmony Lane and fell upon Lucas. He stood between the cabins in his full intimidating statue mode with his right hand behind him holding the machete, whose tip peeked out from between his legs. Rick knew his brain told his feet to move; a command had been issued, yet his feet refused to obey.

"Move to the car." Dale remained stiff and unmoving. Their eyes followed the machete as it grew more erect.

Lucas pulled down the scarves from around his mouth and opened wide, flicking the stump of his tongue at them as the machete reached its full extent.

"Oh shit." Rick realized who the figure standing in front of them was first. His bladder unleashed a warm stream down his leg as he inched his right leg out toward the car in an effort to start running. "It's him."

"There's no way." Dale didn't blink, his eyes

drawn to the figure in front of him. His chest went tight, and like Rick, he felt a rush of warmth spreading in his jeans. Dale fell to his knees, mouth opened in shock.

"Dale...get up." He waited, but Dale remained on his knees, tears running down his face. "Fuck this." Rick shook himself free of his fear and broke into a sprint for the car.

Lucas moved faster. The machete sang as it flew. Rick glanced backwards, hoping Dale had jumped to his feet but found the machete nailed him in the shoulder and sent him to the ground. Before Rick could react, Lucas grabbed him. He fought, flailing his hands wildly at his attacker to no avail. He was thrown down on the scalding hot hood of the car. Rick's cries for Dale to help him were cut short as Lucas's gloved fingers reached into his mouth, filling the cavity with the taste of blood and dirt. He forced Rick's mouth open wider and wider until he'd torn the bottom jaw entirely away. Lucas took ahold of Rick's flopping tongue and ripped the organ from his skull.

Dale cried out, helpless to do anything, as Rick's body fell to the ground in front of the car. His horror-filled eyes locked onto Dale's as the blood from his mouth flowed into tiny rivers through the pieces of gravel. A shadow fell over Dale, and Lucas retrieved the machete, pulling it from him as if he were the stone and Lucas, King Arthur. He held the blade in the air, the sun gleaming off the tip, before he drove it into Dale's crotch, and pushed deep through his body and into the earth underneath.

☠

Dale's pained cries were carried on the breeze through the trees and over the fifty yards to where Tyler stood somber and straight-faced. He was slightly unsettled but happy a lifetime of horror movies, video games (and a night filled with actual dead bodies) had desensitized him. Ty wanted to see the abusers delivered to Lucas.

Jamal stood next to him but kept their back to the unfolding scene. "Is he done?"

Lucas roared triumphantly, holding up the mangled remains of Dale's genitals.

"Yeah, I'd say he is." Ty loved that Chris and Jamal insisted on coming out to the camp with him even though he'd told them they didn't need to join; the plan was his to see through to the end.

Jamal took a breath, and Ty knew they were readying themself for whatever they saw when they turned around. Lucas collected the bodies, one slung over his shoulder and the other dragged along his side. "Where is he always taking them bodies off to?"

"Do you really want to know?" Tyler asked, flashing Jamal a weak smile.

Chris stood back up, wiping the flecks of vomit from his lips. Rick's tongue being removed proved too much for him. "I can't take seeing any more of this shit. Is it over?"

Tyler rubbed his hand across Chris's back. "I think so."

"Girl, you *think*?" Jamal shook their head. "I need something definite, something concrete hunty. Tell me the angry Saltine over there is going sleepy night-night forever."

"Hopefully, he gets to pass on and go to whatever is next and finds peace.

Or maybe he just goes back to sleep." Tyler felt certain the ordeal was over; Lucas's abusers met their demise at his hands. And by the rules of supernatural killers as far as movies had taught him, Tyler figured that equaled a settled score. Either way, he was ready to put Horizons and Lucas behind him. With Jamal next to him, he began to walk away. After a few steps, Ty noticed Chris hadn't moved. He hung behind, still looking out at the camp. "You okay, babe?"

"I was just wondering...what if he's stuck out here roaming Lake Never forever?" Chris's face went sullen, his eyes drooped. Tyler realized as much terror as Lucas had instilled in them over one night, a big dose of sadness came included. "What if...he never gets to leave?"

They remained silent, letting Chris's question hang in the air between the three of them. None of them wanted that fate for Lucas, but the mystery behind what brought him back lingered, and Tyler could offer no certainty.

"If he does have to stay here, roaming, then I feel really sorry for anyone who tries to open this camp again. And"—Tyler held out his open hand, which Chris took in his as the trio made their way back to the car—"any small-minded assholes who want to come out and play in *his* woods.

The End...

About Eric David Roman

Eric David Roman spent twenty years wandering the wrong paths; he tends to get lost a lot (he's from Florida). He worked the wrong jobs (as it turns out, streetwalking is not a profession for just anyone) and avoided his true passion—writing, or as he refers to it, shotgunning sleeves of gluten-free double stuff Oreos in a dark closet whilst crying. After hitting a low point while trapped in retail management hell (a harsh rock bottom), he rearranged his thinking (now with 75 percent less anxiety and depression), got a little spiritual (but isn't all in-your-face about it) and switched his focus fully to writing; well, as much as his gAyDD allows. And now, you're reading his bio, so things are progressing nicely. He is the author of the outrageous novella *Despicable People*, the new novel *Long Night at Lake Never*, and multiple upcoming works. Eric remains socially distant in Northern Virginia (don't stalk him, you'd just be disappointed), where he lives, writes, and loves a mix of all things horror, campy, and queer. He spends the days with his adoring husband and loveable cat (both of whom remain indifferent to his self-proclaimed celebrity).

☠

Printed in Great Britain
by Amazon